Inland Empire

20
06

INLAND EMPIRE

MELISSA ANDERSON

Published in Australia in 2021
by Fireflies Press
www.firefliespress.com

Cover and book design by James Geoffrey Nunn
Typeset by Brett Weekes in Alcalá, by 205TF
Printed and bound by KOPA. First printing.

Distributed by
Idea Books (international) and Books at Manic (Australia)

ISBN: 978-3-9819186-9-4

A catalogue record for this book is available
from the National Library of Australia

The Decadent Editions series is generously
supported by our Publishing Partner
ACMI: the museum of screen culture.

For LKG, my Franklin

The directive is beseeching, mildly bullying, desperate: 'Look at me – and tell me if you've known me before.' It is delivered, more than once, by Laura Dern, the star of David Lynch's *Inland Empire*. Dern plays an actress, Nikki Grace, who, at first blush, appears soigné and imperturbable but who eventually shatters, splintering into multiple personae. She is, per the film's tagline, 'a woman in trouble.' *Inland Empire* is Lynch's tenth feature and his avowed final film. It is not his last or first collaboration with Dern, the writer-director's original blonde.

•

Look at me – and tell me if you've known me before. Isn't this the anxious question, framed as an imperative, that all actors wish to have answered affirmatively as an index of recognition and fame? This snippet of dialogue and others heard in the film become eldritch earworms, slogans of bruised, buffeted souls. *Inland Empire*, like its beloved immediate predecessor, *Mulholland Drive* (2001), the last of Lynch's features to have been shot on celluloid, is about an actress; both films present a sinister, shadow-self of sanitised Hollywood history.

The later movie is the more difficult one to embrace, however much one may admire it. Premiering at the Venice Film Festival in September 2006, *Inland Empire* had a limited release in the United States in December of that year. Met with mixed critical reception, it earned just a little over $4 million globally, a fraction of *Mulholland Drive*'s box-office grosses. The two films have almost invariably been yoked together; in her laudatory review of *Inland Empire*, for example, critic Manohla Dargis nonetheless deemed it the 'evil twin' of *Mulholland Drive*. Running three hours, *Inland Empire*, both visually and thematically, evokes constant dread. Lynch shot it himself, using a Sony camcorder, on muddy, smudgy digital video, a lo-res format that mirrors the movie's begrimed protagonist and her increasingly tenuous grip on reality. The film is the colour of night terrors. Yet despite its overwhelming gloom, *Inland Empire* mesmerises, its pull resulting from the thrills of watching a well-known performer, one long affiliated with this particular director, transform, stretch herself into terrified, terrifying characters. Dern's long, Modigliani-like face has never been more elastic; her mouth becomes a maw, a portal to an annihilating abyss.

In fact, the most distilled depiction of horror in *Inland Empire* arises from the grimace that creeps across Dern's visage during one of Nikki's many deranging moments of existential free fall. Spot-lit as she hurries down, in slow motion, a narrow path – who is she running from? – Nikki pushes right up against the camera; her face, now bathed in a smeary yellow light, fills the frame. From her open mouth, a gruesome rectangle, seems to emerge a scream no less piercing for its silence.

We've seen that look before. In the small-town murder mystery *Blue Velvet* (1986), the inaugural

Lynch-Dern collaboration, the actress, then still a teenager, plays a high school student named Sandy Williams who falls in love with and assists Jeffrey Beaumont, an amateur college-age sleuth. When ingenuous Sandy discovers that her sweetheart is also sexually involved with a psychologically scarred, older chanteuse, Dern contorts her mouth into a fathomless rictus of humiliation and pain, a frown so expansive that it appears taffy-pulled. Dern's aghast expressions in *Blue Velvet* and *Inland Empire* are not unlike the bare-fanged glower of another fair-haired teen, the tortured Laura Palmer, as she speaks from beyond the grave in *Twin Peaks: Fire Walk with Me*, Lynch's 1992 movie prequel to his cult television series. Sandy, Laura, Nikki: each a woman troubled or in trouble, each sending out an SOS via a look of unremitting pain.

•

In his book *Lynch on Lynch*, Chris Rodley writes of the harm inflicted by trying to 'describe' *Mulholland Drive*. 'Words are the movie's enemy,' he declares. Lynch himself has said as much throughout his career. Deflecting questions about *Inland Empire*, the director told the *New York Times*, 'As soon as you put things in words, no one ever sees the film the same way. And that's what I hate, you know. Talking – it's real dangerous.'

This sense of futility, of fatuousness bedevils me as I try to write about *Inland Empire*. To recapitulate the plot of this labyrinthine film would be to replicate the tedium and pointlessness of narrating a dream. I don't want to analyse the film as an enigma to be solved or decoded – the strategy embraced by many criticasters and online listicle-compilers in their discussions of *Mulholland Drive* and *Inland Empire* and countless other films since. Words are my enemy – and probably yours, too.

Yet a synopsis might go as follows: Dern stars as Nikki Grace, an actress who is preparing for a hard-won part in a film called *On High in Blue Tomorrows*, a swampy Southern gothic melodrama in which she – Nikki, that is – plays a character named Susan Blue. Acting opposite Dern, Justin Theroux plays Nikki's co-star, a lothario named Devon Berk; Devon's character in the film within the film has the lubricious appellation Billy Side. Mirroring her character's arc in *On High in Blue Tomorrows*, the married Nikki falls for Devon (who, unlike Billy, is single); Nikki and Susan start to become indistinguishable. Our sense of place also becomes scrambled as the film toggles unexpectedly between Southern California and Łódź; in one scene, Nikki – or is it Susan? – seems to teleport from the Golden State to arrive, still in her ribbed, varicoloured tank top, on a deserted, frigid, snowy street in the Polish city. Even more baffling, some scenes in Poland appear to take place during the 1930s.

Another destabilising element is introduced when Nikki and Devon learn, courtesy of their affable director, Kingsley Stewart (Jeremy Irons), that *On High in Blue Tomorrows* is a remake of a cursed European film called *Vier, Sieben* (Four, Seven; the numbers will appear much later in *Inland Empire*), a production ultimately abandoned after the two leads were murdered. 'Something inside the story,' as Kingsley cryptically explains, seems to have diabolical power. But even the brief description I've provided imposes a cohesion that never quite obtains in Lynch's movie. The most potent précis of *Inland Empire* remains its tagline: a woman in trouble.

•

Even if "making sense" of *Inland Empire* is ultimately futile, that doesn't mean the film isn't legible. It's simply a matter of expanding the notion of authorship. Specifically, Dern – whose gestures, reactions and movements, always pinpoint precise in their immensity, make this bewildering project indelible and even at times lucid – might be thought of as just as much of a creator as Lynch. A co-producer of the movie, Dern also supplied its title: in a conversation with the director, she mentioned that her romantic partner at the time (and later her husband), musician Ben Harper, grew up in the Inland Empire, a region to the east of Los Angeles. (Harper appears, uncredited, as a piano player in the film's closing credits sequence.) Dern's terrifying grimace is the movie's signature. Her stretchy body tautens *Inland Empire*'s viscous, malefic expanse.

I love Lynch's movies and consider him one of the greatest American filmmakers of the past half-century. But his work has been analysed and picked apart for nearly as long, to increasingly diminishing returns (a notable exception being Dennis Lim's superlative, compact book *David Lynch: The Man from Another Place*). I am not interested in writing about *Inland Empire* with an auteurist focus – or at least I don't want that to be my sole method of investigation. What interests me, what seems to be the most fruitful way of approaching this confounding movie is to explore it through the lens of 'acteurism'.

I was first made aware of this term thanks to a recurring film series at the Museum of Modern Art organised under that name by curator Dave Kehr. In his notes for the inaugural acteurist programme, mounted in 2014 and dedicated to the saucy forties B-movie great Ann Sheridan, Kehr explains that the series is 'devoted to actors who were able to develop their screen personalities with sufficient consistency and vivacity that they themselves became vehicles of meaning in their movies.' Other performers saluted in the series have included

Joel McCrea, possessed of an agile nonchalance that served him well in a variety of genres, from the zingy comedies of Preston Sturges to the westerns that dominated the latter part of the actor's career; and Ginger Rogers, renowned not only for her multiple pairings with Fred Astaire but also for the world-weary strivers she played in movies such as Gregory La Cava's *Stage Door* (1937).

As the above list of celluloid icons implies, MoMA's acteurist series has assayed the careers of performers from golden-age Hollywood. But the concept is no less valid when applied to a contemporary performer like Dern, who, in her films with Lynch, especially *Inland Empire*, has been a superb explorer of the vast, murky psychic terrain where innocence mingles with defilement and vice versa – and thus the primary 'vehicle of meaning' for this insoluble 2006 movie. I am put in mind of the proto-acteurist beliefs of the preeminent gay cult film critic Boyd McDonald. In a piece collected in *Cruising the Movies: A Sexual Guide to Oldies on TV*, he wrote of Richard Widmark, a paradigmatic film noir tough guy and one of his favourite performers, that 'he demonstrates the importance of the movie star over the movie and thus the importance of star reviews over mere movie reviews, with their constant complaints about plot.' This seems an especially sound approach when writing a monograph about a film that is exceedingly difficult to parse cogently – that in fact seems purposefully designed to resist meaning being overlaid on it.

Also relevant is this line from the introduction of James Naremore's foundational study *Acting in the Cinema*, which sees the actor as equally important as the film text itself: 'Clearly films depend on a form of communication whereby meanings are *acted out*; the experience of watching them involves not only a pleasure in storytelling but also a delight in bodies and expressive movement, an enjoyment of familiar performing skills, and an interest in players as "real persons".' Later, Naremore makes clear that the very physicality of the performer – 'a series of expressive techniques governing such matters as posture, gesture, and voice, and regulating the entire body as an index of gender, age, ethnicity, and social class' – is crucial to his analysis of cinema acting, and by extension, essential to making sense of a film. In a project as ungraspable as *Inland Empire*, Dern's corporeality functions as the movie's irreducible reality.

I remember something that Lily Tomlin – who rose to fame in the seventies as a comedian known for inhabiting an array of voluble personae – says in Nick Broomfield and Joan Churchill's documentary *Lily Tomlin* (1986), which recounts the numerous tryouts leading up to the Broadway debut of *The Search for Signs of Intelligent Life in the Universe*, the one-woman play written and directed by Jane Wagner, Tomlin's partner in work and love. In the show, Tomlin embodies a dozen or so different characters, a high-wire performing feat similar to Dern's in *Inland Empire*. 'All I have is my voice and my body... to make it believable,' Tomlin laments in the documentary of the challenge she was facing after a snafu-laden tech run-through. What Dern does with her ectomorphic body, her elastic face, her accented speech is indispensable to keeping the spectator tethered, if not held rapt, to the psychic entropy of Lynch's film. To Naremore's emphasis on the performer's corporeal distinctions, though, I would add the following gender-specific corollary, another observation by McDonald: 'Motion pictures are for people who like to watch women.' I've quoted this adage countless times since first reading *Cruising the Movies*, for it so concisely distils my cinephilia. It would also seem to operate as the organising principle of Lynch's otherwise disjointed final feature, a project that puts one woman front and centre for its entire epic runtime.

•

'The actor's life is one of the hardest lives,' Lynch has said. The filmmaker puckishly highlighted the abjection of stardom – or, more specifically, of being a female actor or star – in his larky 'For Your Consideration' Oscar campaign for Dern for Best Actress in the fall of 2006. Lynch, positioned between a live cow and a blown-up still of Dern, sat at the corner of Hollywood Boulevard and La Brea Avenue, amiably chatting with curious passers-by. Where Lynch stationed himself isn't too far from where Nikki (or one of her avatars) bleeds out on the sidewalk, having been stabbed with her own screwdriver by a bedraggled character, who may be a version of Doris Side, Billy's wife in *On High in Blue Tomorrows*, played by Julia Ormond. After Nikki dies, following a seemingly interminable monologue by a young, homeless Japanese woman – one of the more fatiguing episodes in this great but flawed film – the camera pulls back to reveal that the scene we've just witnessed was "shot" by Kingsley, the director of *On High in Blue Tomorrows*.

We are plunged into a mise en abyme, a doubling squared by real-life data. The gore-coated tool stuck into Nikki's guts falls near the star of Dorothy Lamour on the Hollywood Walk of Fame. On November 1, 2010, Dern and her actor parents, Bruce Dern and Diane Ladd, received adjoining stars on this famed stretch of pavement, the first family to have been afforded such treatment. These temporal slippages, these proleptic incidents, bring to mind the admission by another of Nikki's selves, a battered woman who speaks at length to a nearly mute, bespectacled man behind a desk: 'The thing is, I don't know what was before or after.'

•

Born in 1967, Laura Dern is the second child of Ladd and Bruce Dern, who met while doing an Off-Broadway production of Tennessee Williams's *Orpheus Descending* in 1960. That same year they married and welcomed their first daughter, Diane Elizabeth Dern, who died eighteen months later from head injuries after falling into a swimming pool. After her parents divorced in 1969, Laura was raised primarily by her mother and maternal grandmother. In the early seventies, she made her first, uncredited appearances in the movies. You can spot her, for example, in Martin Scorsese's *Alice Doesn't Live Here Anymore* (1974); wearing glasses, she eats an ice cream cone at the counter of Mel's Diner, where Ladd's Flo works as a waitress. Adrian Lyne's *Foxes* (1980) features Dern in her first credited screen role, as a swaggering tween named Debbie, eager to offer advice about birth control. She turned thirteen while filming Lou

Adler's *Ladies and Gentlemen the Fabulous Stains* (1982), in which she plays Jessica, the bassist of a DIY all-girl pop-punk trio. Although Jessica has just a few lines, Dern reveals an immense talent for portraying adolescent emotional extremes: disdain for the adults in her pitiful small town on the one hand, stark terror at what grown-up life has in store on the other – sentiments that the actress would explore more fully in Joyce Chopra's coming-of-age tale *Smooth Talk* (1985), which gave Dern her first lead role.

At age sixteen, Dern won, with her mother's assistance, legal emancipation, allowing her to work the demanding schedule of an adult actor. When she was seventeen, she moved into her own apartment, which she shared with someone then almost twice her age: Marianne Williamson, who would later achieve a different kind of fame, as a spiritual leader and fringe 2020 presidential candidate. Dern enrolled at UCLA, with the ambitious hopes of double majoring in journalism and psychology. She dropped out two days into her first semester, after being offered the role of Sandy in *Blue Velvet*, a film for which she was selected largely owing to her sanguine disposition. Lynch, who, for most of his career, has forsworn the traditional auditioning process when casting his films, met with Dern for a series of informal conversations, some at one of his favourite hangouts, Bob's Big Boy. As the actress recalled in a 2020 interview, 'I know he was looking for someone he believed was really pure. Not in a physical way ... but pure of heart, maybe. ... He needed Sandy, at her root, to be such a believer, so hopeful, such an optimist, and that really is my nature.'

•

In *Blue Velvet*, Sandy first appears as a still, not moving, image: a gold-framed photo of the smiling high school senior rests next to a duck decoy on the home office desk of her police investigator father, with whom Kyle MacLachlan's Jeffrey, a dilettante gumshoe determined to solve a gruesome crime, has just been chatting. As Jeffrey ambles down a suburban sidewalk following his meeting with Detective Williams, Sandy emerges from total darkness, a radiant vision in pink and white – the same colour scheme as her bedroom, oddly dominated by a poster of post-accident Montgomery Clift. 'Are you the one that found the ear?' she asks him. The query suggests that Sandy, despite her cheery mien, also has an appetite for the macabre and for mystery-solving, a trait that transforms her into Jeffrey's part-time accomplice and, not too much later, his girlfriend.

In the course of his snooping, Jeffrey has darker desires awakened when he becomes romantically entangled with the damaged nightclub singer Dorothy Vallens (Isabella Rossellini, in her first major role in English), whom he is trying to rescue from her thralldom to the amyl nitrite-huffing sociopath Frank Booth (Dennis Hopper). When a distraught Jeffrey relays to Sandy the extent of Frank's malevolence, Dern brilliantly executes an aria of moony sincerity as she delivers the film's trickiest bit of dialogue, describing a hopeful dream about robins conquering all sinister forces. Sitting in the driver's seat of her parked car, behind which the organ of a nearby church is audible, Sandy turns away from Jeffrey to recount her vision. Her eyes glance skyward, and her voice, though hushed, increases in excitement, zeal matched by her gesticulating hands:

> For the longest time there was just this darkness. And all of a sudden, thousands of robins were set free. And they flew down and brought this blinding light of love. And it seemed like that love would be the only thing that would make any difference. And it did.

Dern ennobles this hokey avian augury by imbuing it with an unwavering awe – an adolescent's incorruptible faith that righteousness can be restored to a wretched world.

Her earnestness in this scene recalls her guileless wonder in a segment from Peter Bogdanovich's *Mask* – released just the year before *Blue Velvet* – in which she plays a blind girl named Diana who falls in love with Rocky, a boy with a severe craniofacial deformity portrayed by Eric Stoltz. To explain the concept of colours to Diana, Rocky devises a system whereby the varying temperatures of a rock he places in her hands signify a spectrum ranging from red to icy blue. Conveying Diana's fascination, Dern evinces not the slightest bit of mawkishness, emphasising instead her character's emotional and intellectual awakening as she becomes a budding synaesthete.

Although Sandy shares Diana's sunniness, she is far more multifaceted, her innocence complicated by her fervour for intimate knowledge of seamy crimes. Four years later, in Lynch's sexed-up road movie *Wild at Heart* (1990), Dern would play a character who grew up far removed from Sandy's cloistered small-town safety yet is still possessed of her innate goodness: Lula, a streetwise young woman who became brutally aware of life's horrors firsthand at a young age but whose pure love for her ex-con boyfriend, Sailor, makes her an exemplar of sincerity.

Both Sandy and Lula can be thought of as forerunners to the multiple roles Dern inhabits in *Inland Empire*. Fragments of pampered Sandy surface in Nikki, especially in the first thirty minutes of the film, when Nikki appears to us a cossetted figure, attended to by servants in her opulent home and so prim that she objects to the use of the word 'fucking'. The offending term is uttered by an unnamed, hostile, Mitteleuropean-accented neighbour (played by Lynch veteran

Grace Zabriskie), whose eerily portentous, time-scrambling talk – 'If it was tomorrow, you would be sitting over there' – signals one of the film's, and thus Nikki's, first breaks with reality. Lula, in turn, drifts through *Inland Empire,* particularly after Nikki morphs into several different personae, at least two of whom speak in the same Southern drawl as *Wild at Heart*'s violated heroine and share some aspects of her wretched backstory.

In addition to marking the first Lynch-Dern collaboration, *Blue Velvet* also established one of the director's trademark motifs, a noir hallmark that he would explore repeatedly: the dichotomy between a light-haired woman and a dark-haired one, with Sandy the virtuous blonde to Dorothy's immoral brunette. That device is pronounced in *Twin Peaks*, which also introduces another Lynch obsession, doubling. Airing for two seasons on network television from 1990 to 1991, *Twin Peaks* features Sheryl Lee playing not only dead (and blonde) Laura Palmer but also her dark-haired cousin, Maddy Ferguson. Similarly, *Lost Highway* (1997) stars Patricia Arquette times two – one blonde, one brunette. Deploying these seemingly primitive conceits – colour-coded divisions, duplicating – Lynch creates female characters who exist in an infinitely complex realm, the uncanny terrain where archetypes shape-shift into haunted, haunting figures.

•

Doubling itself would be doubled in *Mulholland Drive*, Lynch's gutting romance, split between beautiful wish-fulfilment dream and hideous nightmare. Many of the film's pleasures operate as the inverse of those found in *Inland Empire*. Rather than being spellbound by a famous actress (and Lynch regular) boldly inhabiting a fractured self, we marvel at the performances by two actresses who were then relatively unknown, Naomi Watts and Laura Elena Harring, each working with Lynch for the first time. In this bifurcated film, the ebullient, flaxen-haired actress-hopeful Betty Elms (Watts) – who rescues and becomes enamoured with the brunette amnesiac Rita (Harring) – may or may not be the dreamed-of, ideal self of the wretched character who replaces Betty in the final thirty minutes: unsuccessful actress Diane Selwyn (also Watts), so undone by her break-up with rising star Camilla Rhodes (Harring again) that she hires someone to kill her. Sandy, Dern's cheerful, naïve but determined mystery-solver in *Blue Velvet*, anticipates optimistic – and equally golden-tressed – Betty, who is resolute in piecing together what happened to Rita before she lost her memory.

Mulholland Drive, for its part, has, thanks to a notable headpiece, a semiotic link to *Inland Empire* and *Twin Peaks: The Return*, the 2017 Showtime limited series that reunited Dern with both Lynch and MacLachlan. In that show, she plays Diane, the factotum and confidante of MacLachlan's Special FBI Agent Dale Cooper – casting that suggests an oblique reprise of their crime-solving duo in *Blue Velvet*. (The G-man in *The Return* has two other incarnations: Coop, an evil doppelgänger; and the bumbling Dougie Jones, a tulpa – that is, an imaginary being that attains corporeal reality.) Diane, we eventually learn, has also been duplicated. And her blondeness – at least in one of her manifestations – is maximised: the secretary sports a blindingly white Louise Brooks-style bob, a coiffure and colour that's a near replica of the platinum wig donned by Rita shortly before her love scene with Betty in *Mulholland Drive*. In *Inland Empire*, the blonde Nikki/Susan is stabbed in the guts by the dark-haired Doris avatar. As Nikki/Susan bleeds out near the iconic intersection of Hollywood and Vine, the homeless Japanese woman regales her with a shambolic story about her friend Niko, who owns a blonde wig that makes her look 'just like a movie star'; Niko, in that very peruke, will appear in the closing minutes.

•

Inland Empire calls for Dern to be not just doubled but quadrupled. In addition to Nikki and Susan, she inhabits two other unnamed personalities that appear to be offshoots of the latter, since they, like Susan, speak (usually) in a sodden Southern accent. (It is the intonation of Dern's own mother, born and raised in Mississippi, who has a pulpy cameo in *Inland Empire* as the venomous host of a gossipy TV chat programme, *The Marilyn Levens Starlight Celebrity Show*. Ladd had previously worked with her daughter and Lynch in *Wild at Heart*, a film, in a twist on the director's usual colour-coded signifying, dense with evil blondes, not least Ladd's Marietta Fortune, mother of Dern's Lula; Mama Marietta's flamboyantly arranged golden locks are just one indicator of her lunacy.) One of these putative Susan subsidiaries is the bruised woman, mentioned earlier, who recounts her autobiography – a life filled with torment and abuse that she is determined to avenge – to a lumpy, esentially speechless male interlocutor. The other is a resident of a small ramshackle house, which I imagine to be somewhere in the Inland Empire.

It's difficult to keep count of Dern's various incarnations, and attempting to do so detracts from one of the film's key satisfactions. Watching an actress play an actress – especially one as gifted as Dern, in a project designed to obfuscate if not shatter entirely boundaries between self and other, reality and fantasy – ignites an unmooring, yet not unpleasing, sense of ontological chaos in the viewer.

This fizzy derangement also takes hold in *Mulholland Drive* but from a different perspective. As we watch Watts – whose career up to that point had been dominated by supporting roles in largely forgotten movies – play an aspiring and seemingly unpromising actress, our senses are scrambled further when Betty reveals her heretofore unfathomable talents during an audition. At this tryout, Betty – matched with a much older, leathery, lecherous scene partner played by Chad Everett, a ubiquitous presence on US television in the sixties and seventies – elevates sub-soap-operatic dialogue involving blackmail, family betrayal and a clandestine affair into an electrifying moment of ravenous desire and velvety menace. Writing about this scene for *Film Quarterly*, the scholar and screenwriter George Toles noted, 'The only earthly identity that might be strong enough to undo death is that of an actress on the verge of stardom.' The observation applies doubly: to the real Naomi Watts and the fictional Betty Elms.

•

By the time of *Inland Empire*, Dern had been a star for twenty years, her celebrity dating back to her breakthrough performances in *Mask* and *Smooth Talk*. Less than a decade later, she achieved global fame owing to her principal role as a paleobotanist in the Steven Spielberg dino blockbuster *Jurassic Park* (1993). Nikki, we surmise, isn't a neophyte like Betty but more like the woman portraying her: a veteran of Hollywood. Nikki's career appears to be in a bit of a slump, however; during the first read-through of *On High in Blue Tomorrows*, Kingsley assures her that the film 'is a star-maker if I ever saw one.' *Inland Empire*'s connection to *Mulholland Drive* – as the second part of a dual project (if an accidental one) about actresses – is underscored by the fact that Watts and Harring appear in the later film. Their faces hidden underneath enormous rabbit heads, both performers (in addition to Scott Coffey, another *Mulholland Drive* alum) portray the bunny-human hybrids who star in the bleak, laugh-tracked TV sitcom that a lachrymose Polish woman, identified in the credits only as Lost Girl (Karolina Gruszka), watches in the room of a Łódź hotel. (In these leporine sequences, the characters flatly deliver gnomic dialogue at once foreboding and inane; the line 'I have a secret,' for instance, is followed by 'There have been no calls today.' The segments originally premiered in 2002 on davidlynch.com, a website that the filmmaker enthusiastically launched in late 2001.)

More beguilingly, Harring appears at the very end of *Inland Empire*, one of several women (who also include Nastassja Kinski) lounging in a luxe hotel lobby. Harring seductively blows a kiss to Dern, who returns the gesture, though hers has less erotic heat. The exchange, with its sapphic frisson, calls up the devastating romance between Betty/Diane and Rita/Camilla. (The same-sex coquetry additionally conjures memories of Dern's performance, as a lesbian newscast producer, opposite Ellen DeGeneres in the infamous coming-out episode of TV's *Ellen* in 1997.)

Harring's presence and her flirtation with Dern in the final scene also points to a painful reality: despite her extraordinary performance in *Mulholland Drive* – in which, in her incarnation as Camilla, she plays an in-demand movie actress – Harring's career never really took off after the 2001 film. Dispiritingly, among Harring's more high-profile assignments in the five years between *Mulholland Drive* and *Inland Empire* was starring in the 2003 remake of the rat-philic horror movie *Willard*. (Watts, especially in the decade following *Mulholland Drive*, would have much more success than her co-star, though solidly A-lister status has largely eluded her. Since 2010, one of her most notable performances has been as Janey-E Jones, Dougie Jones's spouse, in *Twin Peaks: The Return*.) That blown kiss between Dern and Harring – two actresses who will forever be associated with Lynch – acts as a kind of leveller between a celebrity and a performer whose promise has never quite been realised. *The actor's life is one of the hardest lives*: Lynch proves himself a paragon of black-hearted empathy and compassion in his actress diptych, a hinged altarpiece to imperilled women at once brutal and tender.

•

In his *Film Quarterly* essay, Toles makes an astute observation that is pertinent to any discussion of *Inland Empire*: '[Lynch] illuminates how rife with contradictions our engagement with any star performance is, yet shows how an awareness of contradictions, far from rescuing us from naïve involvement, can increase the likelihood of wholesale surrender to the acting hoax.' As an example of this scenario, Toles, describing Betty's stunning success at her audition – which is inseparable from Watts's bedazzling of the spectator – writes, 'The full throttle romantic acting of the old Hollywood school penetrates our defenses just as we are most confident that we understand the limitations – the unembarrassed obviousness – of this kind of acting.'

It is precisely this kind of acting that distinguishes Nikki's performance in *On High in Blue Tomorrows*. Dern, an actress playing an actress determined to gain more notice, seamlessly slips into haut-Southern-gothic mode during the read-through and eventual shooting of the film within the film. Superficially, Nikki's acting in *On High in Blue Tomorrows* recalls that of Elizabeth Taylor in the 1958 movie version of *Cat on a Hot Tin Roof*, one of three Tennessee Williams adaptations to star La Liz, who reliably elevated the playwright's emotional maximalism to florid new heights. (There's something inside the story: as it happens, Dern is a distant relative of the playwright, for her mother is Williams's cousin.) But crucially, Nikki Grace as Susan Blue – which is a roundabout way of saying Dern – knows just how to calibrate the melodramatics required of her role. Nikki's fantastic in the part because she tweaks and updates 'acting of the old Hollywood school'; in one scene of Kingsley's movie, she tempers a heavily flirtatious exchange with insouciant gum-chewing. She's so good, in fact, that viewers find it just as difficult as Nikki does to distinguish where she ends and Susan begins.

Much of the spectator's astonishment at Betty's transformation in *Mulholland Drive* – from a sunny, sexless actress-hopeful who had previously evinced little promise while running her lines with Rita the morning of her audition to a deftly instinctual performer exuding a tremendous carnal aura – hinges on the fact that the then-little-known Watts had no established persona. The opposite scenario applies to Dern in *Inland Empire*. She is known to us (*Look at me – and tell me if you've known me before*) owing in no small part to her earlier work with Lynch. *Inland Empire* originated in a fourteen-page monologue that Lynch wrote for the actress, after the two ran into each other outside his house – they had recently become neighbours – and expressed an eagerness to work together again. Lynch devised the scene solely as a one-off experiment, with no thought of a film in mind. But after shooting the monologue (a session that totalled four hours, done in 'trancelike' 45-minute takes) in February 2003 on a set constructed in the director's painting studio, he was so impressed by Dern's performance that the idea for a feature-length movie, one that would never have a final screenplay, took root.

As it appears in *Inland Empire*, the monologue that served as the movie's genesis is preceded by the roughed-up Nikki/Susan avatar who delivers it – who, for the sake of simplicity, I'll call the Avenging Angel from here on – hesitantly walking up the stairs of a decaying building. Dressed in business-casual attire, she sits at a desk. In her right hand she clutches a screwdriver, in her left, a pocketbook. She has a black eye and a bruised mouth. Across from her is a bespectacled man, stout, about thirty years old. (Identified in the final credits as Mr. K, he is played by Erik Crary, one of Lynch's assistants.) 'So I was told you can help me,' she says – guidance that will prove wildly off the mark. He listens, but not attentively. He asks the Avenging Angel only one question: 'Were you, in fact, seeing another man?' He could be a confessor, but one who offers no absolution. Or perhaps he's a psychotherapist, his fecklessness reflecting Lynch's notorious aversion to the talking cure, in his view a potential killer of creativity, unlike the generative Transcendental Meditation, which the director has practiced every day since 1973 and requires silence. (Lynch: 'Talking – it's real dangerous.')

Despite – or maybe because of – this strange man's taciturnity and lack of affect, the Avenging Angel recapitulates at length a gruesome saga, which just so happens to be the story of her life: 'There was this man I once knew. His name was – it doesn't matter what his name was.' If proper nouns are insignificant, easily dispensed with, does that mean she's an unreliable narrator? 'I gouged a man's eye out when I was fifteen once; he was tryin' to rape me,' she continues. Chopped up, this soliloquy is distributed throughout the movie, mostly in its latter half; *Inland Empire* itself was shot in fits and starts over three years. As Lynch explained in a *New York Times* feature, there was no cohesive vision for the project: 'I never saw any whole, W-H-O-L-E. I saw plenty of holes, H-O-L-E-S. But I didn't really worry. I would get an idea for a scene and shoot it, get another idea and shoot that. I didn't know how they would relate.'

Sixteen years had elapsed since *Wild at Heart*, Dern and Lynch's prior film. During that decade and a half, Dern worked with a wide range of film-makers, including Martha Coolidge (*Rambling Rose*, 1991); Spielberg; Clint Eastwood (*A Perfect World*, 1993); Alexander Payne (*Citizen Ruth*, 1996); and Robert Altman (*Dr. T and the Women*, 2000). But she had never (and still has never) collaborated with another director as many times as she had with Lynch. With a part – or parts – written expressly for her, the confounding *Inland Empire* is certainly a star vehicle, if a perverse one, a showcase for Dern's extraordinary ability to ground Lynch's arcana and bizarreries in all-too-real human emotions: lust, grief, fear.

An avant-garde experiment, an experiment in terror, *Inland Empire* was an audacious project even for an auteur considered Hollywood's paradigmatic outré filmmaker. But the risk was surely greater for Dern, who appears in nearly every scene of this three-hour phantasmagoria, who must inhabit multiple characters, all in a state of psychic disintegration. Throughout the film, the actress's visage is warped and torqued, a distortion abetted by Lynch's use of murky video, and her body is battered and contused. In several segments, Dern utters not a word, notably when Nikki/Susan slowly expires on Hollywood Boulevard; in that moment, she astoundingly communicates, by opening her mouth just a little wider or narrowing her eyes slightly, the unimaginable loneliness of dying while surrounded by largely unconcerned strangers. Conversely, in Dern's more voluble scenes, as in the long soliloquy, her impeccably calibrated inflections make us fully aware of the potency of speech – here an act that not only helps this dejected confessant make sense of her life but may in fact be prolonging it, keeping her away from the woman who's out to kill her. Again I think of Tomlin's words: all Dern has is her voice and her body to make it believable.

Rather than find the erratic, stop-start method of the three-year shoot discombobulating, Dern embraced its unconventional progression: 'It's unbelievably freeing. You're not sure where you're going or even where you've come from. You can only be in the moment,' she explained in that *Times* piece mentioned above. Dern described how she conceptualised the role: 'I thought of it as playing a broken or dismantled person, with these other people leaking out of her brain.' Catherine Deneuve's performance as a timid young woman inexorably sliding into madness in Roman Polanski's *Repulsion* (1965) served as a guide. (To my mind, that film, the first in English for both its Polish director and its French star – another paradigm of blondeness – forms an oblique kinship with *Inland Empire*, as it bears Deneuve's acteurist stamp just as much as Polanski's auteurist signature. Deneuve's plunge into glacial, homicidal schizophrenia in the movie marks the beginning of a roughly decade-long period in which the actress would cultivate one of the most enduring aspects of her persona: the exquisite blank slate, often defiled, onto whom viewers could assign all sorts of psychosexual depravities. Another connection: Polanski is the most famous alumnus of the National Film School in Łódź, the city where some of *Inland Empire* was shot. Leon Niemczyk, who starred as the macho, ultimately cuckolded husband in Polanski's debut feature, 1962's *Knife in the Water*, has a small role in *Inland Empire* as one of three elderly Poles, seemingly mob-type dons.)

Despite their oddities, *Blue Velvet* and *Wild at Heart*, Dern's two previous films with Lynch, follow a fairly straightforward narrative arc. For *Inland Empire*, the most free-associative, nonlinear movie in the director's singular corpus, the actress must repeatedly perform the fragmenting or slippage of multiple identities. It isn't the first Lynch film to demand this feat of one of its performers; 'the pattern of role confusion', as Toles calls it, shapes *Lost Highway* and *Mulholland Drive* and can be found as far back as *Twin Peaks*. But those earlier projects are all, to varying degrees, anchored by a temporal scaffolding that is nearly nonexistent in *Inland Empire*. Viewers of the film have little sense of its chronology; more to the point, Dern's personae also can't distinguish past, present or future. 'The thing is, I don't know what was before or after. I don't know what happened first,' the Avenging Angel tells her interlocutor. 'It's a story that happened yesterday. But I know it's tomorrow,' Nikki, beginning to merge with Susan, declares.

•

In a film structured by psychic and temporal unmooring, Dern must consistently fall apart but not completely shatter. How does she do this? As I've stated earlier, Dern – through her loose-limbed, linguine-thin body, her pliant face, her talent for modulated surfeit – makes this bewildering movie legible, lucid. I return to Naremore, who proposes that 'realist acting amounts to an effort at sustaining opposing attitudes toward the self, on the one hand trying to create the illusion of unified, individualized personality, but on the other suggesting that character is subject to division or dissolution into a variety of social roles.'

Dern's performance is all the more astonishing for her consistent maintaining of 'realist acting' in a movie that exists at the extreme margins of narrative filmmaking, that is predictable only in its irrationality. That is to say, Dern brilliantly succeeds at creating a cohesive illusion of a woman in trouble, even if that woman is fractured into four different selves. But to delineate the process of *how* Dern manages this demanding feat and, in the process, ensorcells the audience is to risk trotting out banalities. Once again, words are my enemy, for trying to describe the alchemy of acting – of Dern's acting – proves even more hazardous a task than recounting what "happens". 'There was clearly a mystery, as there always is – there's a mystery to solve as the actor in the story,' Dern told me during a phone interview in 2006, when I asked her how she approached her character(s) in the film. To best honour Dern's performance, I find myself tempted to let the mystery stand.

•

An intelligent 2019 profile of the actress for the *New York Times Magazine*, by the critic and novelist Christine Smallwood, offers one way of analysing Dern's unique talent. 'Some actresses are stymied by a fear of excess or wanting to control how they will look, but Dern never holds back,' she notes. 'Her performances are so naked, her characters so un-self-aware, that you sometimes feel that you shouldn't be watching them at all.'

While Dern's raw acting may be so overwhelming that the instinct is to look away, Nikki (and others) insist that we keep our gaze steady. 'It's me, Devon. It's me, Nikki! *Look at me, you fucker*,' she exhorts her co-star during sex. The carnal command is another way of saying, 'Look at me – and tell me if you've known me before,' the most tenacious of *Inland Empire*'s refrains. While fucking, they both seem to slip in and out of their *On High in Blue Tomorrows* characters. Perhaps, in demanding to be seen, Nikki loses sight of herself. Or perhaps I've lost sight of Nikki: Dern's lust in this segment so vividly evokes Lula's sexual hunger in *Wild at Heart* – a film punctuated by her bouts of vigorous rutting with Nicolas Cage's Sailor – that I start to think of Lula as yet another of Nikki's personalities. Perhaps, after staring at, scrutinising Dern so intently, any writer – this writer – who tries to make sense of her mysteries will inevitably follow blind alleys.

•

Descriptors like 'unbearably vulnerable', 'messy' and 'deeply flawed' are often applied to the characters Dern plays; the words certainly pertain to Nikki. But these adjectives don't really offer detail so much as serve as shorthand for the metaphysics of Dern's performing style – one that embraces emotional surplus.

Then again, the very description of acting techniques – especially those that derive from the Method, which demands that its practitioners probe and inhabit the emotional lives of their characters – often seems clotted with hazy language. In her thoroughly researched piece, Smallwood notes the prominence of Method institutions in Dern's family: both of her parents studied at the Actors Studio, and Dern, at the age of nine, took classes at the Lee Strasberg Theatre and Film Institute. Sandra Seacat, Dern's acting teacher of more than thirty years, was also trained in the Method, though her pedagogy, as Smallwood details, is slightly different. Seacat first instructs her charges to write a letter to themselves – a missive that might begin, 'Dear Inner Self, if it is your will, please reveal to me in a dream tonight, the inner truth of this character that is in me, this part of me that's the character.' This talismanic dream is then brought to a workshop, where the actor, per Smallwood, 'might perform rituals based on it or cast other actors to perform it.' Seacat considers the artist 'a shaman, a wounded healer', one with the power to psychically cure the audience. Of her work with Seacat, Dern has enthused, 'It's just so beautiful, to consider [acting] as an opportunity to heal oneself and others through questioning the complications of being human, whatever that means, not in some, you know, preachy way, but in a genuine way.'

That language is easy to ridicule. It calls to mind the gauzy instructions of the director at Betty's audition scene in *Mulholland Drive*, who gives her and her roué scene partner these inane prompts: 'Don't play it for real, until it gets real' and 'The two of them... with themselves.'

To find the processes behind such great acting witless and woo-woo leads to another linguistic impasse: if I am averse to vapid pop-psychology terms like 'wounded healer', how can I intelligently parse what Dern does in *Inland Empire*? My models for this endeavour are those whose lapidary assessments of actresses have endured for decades. In the two-page 'The Face of Garbo' from *Mythologies*, Roland Barthes illuminates the icon's appeal with aperçus like this: 'Garbo offered to one's gaze a sort of Platonic Idea of the human creature, which explains why her face is almost sexually undefined, without however leaving one in doubt.' In a 1954 précis on the same actress, the British theatre critic Kenneth Tynan adroitly deployed simile to anatomise

Garbo's allure: 'To watch her is to achieve direct, cleansed perception of something which, like a flower or a fold of silk, is raptly, unassertively and beautifully itself.' And here is McDonald on noir demigoddess Gloria Grahame:

> [She] is a high school boy's dream of cool, of real, effortless masculinity as opposed to the effort to act masculine made by her co-star in *In a Lonely Place* (1950), a poseur named 'Humphrey Bogart'. She had the sullen, bored walk and talk of someone who can't be shocked, isn't afraid and just doesn't give a shit.

This kind of evocative and economical prose gives a concept as highly subjective and gossamer as "star presence" – which is another way of describing an actor's keen intelligence before the camera, the kind of acumen Dern exhibits – the ballast it needs to seem meaningful and comprehensible. A contemporary writer who excels at this kind of pinpoint analysis is Gary Indiana, who, in a 1990 Q&A with Dern for *Interview*, catalogues her gifts with clarity. 'She has charted the territory where innocence and dark reality meet and mutate into unpredictable forms of life,' Indiana writes. Of the characters

Dern has played, he notes, 'They contain lurking contradictions, mixed feelings, the jumble of motives and impulses present in every person. ... [In *Wild at Heart*] Dern's performance is something to burn your fingers on – raunchy and passionate and anxious and sweet.'

To continue Indiana's felicitous metaphor, Dern's performance in *Inland Empire* is something to char your skin all over, to melt your mind. Contra Sandra Seacat – and Dern – it doesn't heal. The actress is pure flame, a blaze that she adjusts from raging conflagration to guttering flicker. But is this language also too opaque, as silly as the notion of the wounded healer?

Once more I return to Toles, who, in his essay, remains besotted, pleasingly befuddled by 'the still inexplicable primitive rite that is cinema'. Words aren't necessarily his enemy, but he knows when to acknowledge uncertainty, to stop analysing, to succumb to ineffable awe. He poses generative, if rhetorical, questions:

> A moving-picture image somehow acquires enough living dimension to swallow the credulous viewer whole. How is it we

invest these dubious framed reflections
with so much embracing power? How
many 'real' sights and sounds get through
to us with such potent immediacy?

Perhaps we can be swallowed whole (W-H-O-L-E) because we invest so much psychic, at times libidinal, energy in the people we see before us on the screen. 'Cinema is public fantasy that engages spectators' particular, private scripts of desire and identification,' film scholar Patricia White writes in *Uninvited: Classical Hollywood Cinema and Lesbian Representability*. Sometimes these scripts are rewritten. Sometimes they are discarded entirely in favour of improvisation. To watch Dern play a woman (or women) in trouble is to be any combination of turned on, terrified, dumbfounded, stupefied.

•

Dern's recent success has been greeted with that most tedious of social media salutes, the portmanteau hashtag: #Dernaissance, in this case. The term took off in 2017, the year the actress turned fifty, and the year that saw her in prominent roles in enormous franchise hits like *Star Wars: The Last Jedi* and the tony television series *Big Little Lies* and *Twin Peaks: The Return*. In 2019, Dern appeared as Marmee, the endlessly empathetic matriarch in Greta Gerwig's adaptation of *Little Women,* and had a scene-stealing role as a ruthless divorce attorney in Noah Baumbach's *Marriage Story*. For that performance, Dern won an Academy Award, her first, for Best Supporting Actress. She richly deserves these accolades and this renewed admiration, which she has invariably acknowledged with utmost grace. At an age when most actresses would have seen their opportunities shrivel up, she may now be at the peak of her fame.

But I wonder what is lost or tamed when a ferociously talented, protean performer receives this kind of popular and professional recognition. Does *Inland Empire*'s release in the middle of the aughts – a relatively lacklustre decade for Dern, who, although as active as ever, had few, if any, roles of note during those years, Lynch's movie notwithstanding – imbue her performance as an actress desperate to land a leading role with that much more pathos? Did this comparatively humdrum period for Dern – during which she gave birth to her two children, in 2001 and 2004, events that would have affected her ability to work – provide the ideal circumstances for her to take on such an audacious project? Would she agree to a part as unhinged as Nikki Grace now that she is the inaugural recipient of *Vulture*'s honourary degree – a 'tribute' (if a dubious one) bestowed on her in November 2019 and a fatuous metric, much like that hashtag, of her wide acclaim? Dern was thirty-nine when *Inland Empire* premiered. Her triumphs, whether critical or commercial, of the eighties and nineties were long behind her, and the project that was instrumental in paving the way for her recent career efflorescence – the HBO series *Enlightened*, which ran from 2011 to 2013 – was five years away.

•

Inland Empire, like *Mulholland Drive*, takes its title from a Southern California place name. The former is a landlocked region adjacent to Los Angeles, the latter a 34-kilometre stretch of road that snakes through the Hollywood Hills and affords spectacular views of the Los Angeles Basin and the Hollywood sign. Both films, as I mentioned earlier, present a sordid view of SoCal's most prominent industry: moviemaking. They continue a theme explored in Lynch's *Lost Highway*, a neo-noir that takes the adult film industry as one of its subjects and which was the first of the director's movies to explicitly survey Los Angeles, where he has lived since 1970.

In their explorations of stardom's seamier side, the three films recall Kenneth Anger's two *Hollywood Babylon* books: chronicles, strewn with a fair share of myths, that are rife with vile scandals and myriad abjection. In *Lost Highway*, as the critic Nick Pinkerton has pointed out, the *Babylon*-ian aspects emerge via casting, whether in the primary or secondary roles: performers as disparate as Balthazar Getty, Richard Pryor, Gary Busey and Natasha Gregson Wagner either had been involved in high-profile opprobrium by the time of filming or were descendants of those who had been tarnished by disgrace. Others in the cast would be caught up in lurid events a few years after the movie's release, notably Robert Blake – the film's terrifying, vampiric Mystery Man – who was charged with the 2001 murder of his second wife. To date, *Lost Highway* is the last film of his career. (Eerily, the Blake case mirrors the most notorious of all L.A. trials: that of O.J. Simpson, which Lynch has acknowledged as an influence on the movie.)

Emphasising the torturous lives, the constant misery of actresses, *Mulholland Drive* and *Inland Empire* redound to the most paradigmatic of the tawdry tales in Anger's books: the grisly 1947 murder, still unsolved, of aspiring actress Elizabeth Short, alias the Black Dahlia, in southern Los Angeles. 'The Dahlia's connection with the movie industry was marginal, more of an unrealized dream than anything else,' Anger writes in *Hollywood Babylon II*. 'Like thousands of others, she had been drawn to the area "to break into movies". Her story belongs to L.A.'s Shadowland, a twilight zone haunted by the mystery of her murder to this day.'

Psycho-geographically, 'L.A.'s Shadowland' is precisely where *Mulholland Drive* and *Inland Empire* unfold, the films possessed by the ghost of the Black Dahlia. Short's mutilated body is evoked by the rotting corpse that Betty and Rita discover in their quest to piece together amnesiac Rita's identity. That female cadaver will be joined by two others, followed by the offscreen offing of Camilla, set in motion by Diane, who is deranged by heartache and professional envy; and Diane's suicide in the movie's final minutes, the termination of a life made unbearable by grief, rage and humiliation.

Short's severed corpse had been drained of blood, leaving her skin ghostly white – a hue similar to wastrel Diane's pallor and the Avenging Angel's wan, bruised flesh in *Inland Empire*, her complexion washed out even more by the movie's sludgy video. The corners of Short's mouth had been cut up to her ears, creating an effect known as a Glasgow smile – a terrifying disfiguration mimicked by Dern's outsize grimace as she lopes in slo-mo toward the camera.

Throughout *Inland Empire*, a Greek chorus of nine young women, possibly sex workers, appears, alternately taunting, advising or consoling Nikki/Susan. They also echo her distraught catchphrase, demanding, 'Look at us – and tell us if you've known us before.' (One of these women is played by Emily Stofle, who married Lynch in 2009.) Are/were these women, à la Elizabeth Short, à la Betty Elms and Diane Selwyn, also aspiring actresses? Short, who was dead by the age of twenty-two, arrived in Los Angeles six months before her murder. In the media frenzy following her killing, she was rumoured to have been a prostitute; newspapers called her a 'man-crazy adventuress' and quoted her housemate's avowal that Short 'loved to prowl' Hollywood Boulevard. Are all women who come to Southern California to make it in the movie business doomed to become 'lost in the marketplace', per the bizarre allegory delivered to Nikki by her menacing neighbour at the beginning of *Inland Empire*? The buying and selling of an actress's body, her soul, is the most baleful kind of commerce, *Mulholland Drive* and *Inland Empire* suggest, one that too often leads to psychic, if not actual, death.

•

The savage demise of Short and the degradation of Nikki and her antecedents in *Mulholland Drive* exist on a continuum of brutalities and humiliations endured by actresses or actress-hopefuls that exploded into wider view after Harvey Weinstein's downfall in the fall of 2017. Weinstein had been the long-ruling potentate of Shadowland, a reign that began in the late eighties with Miramax's ascendance. His crimes and the general culture of abasement of women he perpetuated had been tolerated or overlooked for decades. He is a member of a despicable fraternity: infamous studio heads, like Harry Cohn and other grandees of Hollywood's golden age, who violated the girls and women hoping to secure – or to continue – their acting careers. (Shortly after the Weinstein story broke, in fact, Ladd recalled being groped by Cohn when she was seventeen.) A fragment from the macabre fable recounted by Nikki's Slavic-accented neighbour echoes in my head. The plot of this 'old tale', as she calls it, is simple: 'A little boy went out to play... evil was born and followed the boy.' An image is conjured: Weinstein and his brethren, past, present and future, romping around Shadowland, treating with impunity actresses of any age as their toys.

•

During the Avenging Angel's long monologue – a soliloquy teeming with tales of imperilment, sexual violence and death – Dern speaks in an especially furry Southern accent, her *g*'s aggressively dropped: 'My husband, he's fuckin' hidin' somethin',' she tells the lumpy, bespectacled man. 'He was actin' all fuckin' weird one night before he left. He was talkin' this foreign talk and tellin' loud fuckin' stories.' The voice and the sordid anecdote remind me of something: the climactic scene in Alfred Hitchcock's *Marnie* (1964), when Minnesota-born Tippi Hedren, recounting her character's childhood trauma – an incident involving a seaman played by Dern's father – slips into a wobbly Southern accent, the dialect of Marnie's impoverished upbringing.

A similarly erratic enunciation marks the line delivery of the British-born Julia Ormond, who also plays a cleaved character in *Inland Empire* – Doris Side in *On High in Blue Tomorrows* and Nikki/Susan's murderer – and speaks in a Southern accent, one less steady than Dern's. Curiously, Ormond does not deploy this distinctive mode of speech in a scene set at the elegant home Doris shares with Billy, even though his words are coated in a thick drawl; posh Doris speaks with a flat American-patrician diction. But as the killer, outfitted in a grimy T-shirt and cut-off jeans, Ormond stretches out her vowels and elides consonants. As it does for the Avenging Angel and Marnie, the idiom signals abject white womanhood.

Ormond's presence in a film about the destabilising life of an actress has a special resonance. In 1995, there was, according to the *New York Times*, 'the inescapable belief among those around her that she may soon be a movie star.' That same year, she played opposite Harrison Ford in a remake of the romantic comedy *Sabrina* and graced the British cover of *Vanity Fair*, which dubbed her 'the next Audrey Hepburn', a proclamation that essentially killed her career; the half-decade preceding *Inland Empire* had been especially fallow for the actress. Shortly after that film's release, Lynch's oldest child, Jennifer, gave Ormond a succulent lead role in *Surveillance* (2008), a gory thriller that, although little-seen, was also a comeback of sorts for its director: it was the first film Jennifer Lynch helmed since the pillorying she received for her feature debut, the amputee fantasia *Boxing Helena* (1993). Playing a steely FBI agent investigating mass slaughter in a small town, Ormond throws herself into the role with the abandon of an actress who has nothing left to lose, adroitly navigating a part that demands boss-lady butchness, inner-child woundedness and id-explosive perversion.

Three years after *Surveillance*, Ormond had a small part as Vivien Leigh in Simon Curtis's dopey *My Week with Marilyn* (2011), about the making of *The Prince and the Showgirl*, the 1957 romantic comedy starring Laurence Olivier and Marilyn Monroe, who are played, with equally enervating avidity, by Kenneth Branagh and Michelle Williams. I mention this otherwise forgettable movie for one reason: a screening of an early version of *My Week with Marilyn* for a festival selection committee that I was a member of occasioned my only meeting with Weinstein, whose company both produced and distributed the film.

Unsurprisingly, he hectored and insulted my four colleagues and me. Huddled close to Weinstein were at least three adjutants, all women, their faces frozen in alarming, fearful smiles. When not bullying my cohort, he boasted of the superfluous changes he was going to insist Curtis make. Thinking back on this encounter a decade later, I see a sick irony in the sovereign of Shadowland bringing into the world yet another worthless project on Monroe, who has been the subject of endless necrophilic attention ever since her death, from an overdose of barbiturates at age thirty-six, in 1962.

Before *Twin Peaks*, in fact, Lynch and Mark Frost, that show's co-creator, had been working on a Monroe feature, ultimately abandoned, called *Goddess*. 'It's hard to say exactly what it is about Marilyn Monroe, but the woman-in-trouble thing is part of it. It's not just the woman-in-trouble thing that pulls you in, though. It's more that some women are real mysterious,' Lynch has said of the icon. *Goddess* may have died, but the Goddess lived on in Lynch's oeuvre: 'You could say that Laura Palmer is Marilyn Monroe, and that *Mulholland Drive* is about Marilyn Monroe, too. Everything is about Marilyn Monroe,' he noted. The totemic blonde, Monroe eventually succumbed to psychic terror as overwhelming as that which deranges another flaxen-haired performer, Nikki Grace.

•

During a visit to Kiev in November 2017 to launch a branch of his charity organisation, the David Lynch Foundation, which funds the teaching of Transcendental Meditation in schools, the director, when asked, vaguely addressed Weinstein's abuses and sexual harassment in general by summoning the Golden Rule: 'We are supposedly judged by how we treat our fellow man'. He continued:

> In a perfect world, if you're about to do something to someone, you should think, 'Would I like this same thing to be done to me?' If the answer is no, then that's not a good thing to do. If the answer is 'Yes, I'd like that very much,' then that's a good thing to do. That works for all avenues of life.

Refusing to perform outrage and indignation, Lynch fell back on his cornpone-sage persona – Maharishi by way of Missoula, Montana – cheerily reminding us of the ethic of responsibility.

Though both *Mulholland Drive* and *Inland Empire* precede the Weinstein scandal by more than a decade, Lynch made a rather transparent dig at the corpulent movie magnate in the earlier film. A bulky thug – who looks like a near double of Weinstein – arrives at the home of preening auteur Adam Kesher (played by Theroux) and, not finding him there, roughs up the director's adulterous wife and her lover. Yet the lampoon alludes not to the producer's gross sexual misconduct – behaviour that had been an open secret for decades but never explicitly addressed – but to his bullying, a part of the Weinstein persona for which the mogul was outrageously proud and thus something of an easy target.

•

How much of Dern's conception of Nikki and the 'other people leaking out of her brain' was influenced by what she experienced or witnessed over the course of her long career, begun when she was a child? Is it too far-fetched to say that the profession of acting for Nikki (and her Lynchian fore-sisters) is *trauma*? Once again I return to Toles. He writes: 'For Lynch, the fact of a character's conspicuous fabrication is no safeguard against real hurt. He often reserves his greatest torments for those most deeply enfolded in artifice, as though the artificial (in its nearness to dream) were the natural seedbed for trauma.'

Just as conspicuously fabricated – arguably by Dern more so than Lynch – and as enfolded in artifice are the several personalities that emerge from Nikki's shattered psyche. 'Watchin' it, like in a dark theatre,' the Avenging Angel tells her ineffectual interlocutor, the antecedent for 'it' being her miserable life, made even more gruelling after an unimaginable loss. And there is no darker theatre than that which hosts Nikki's dreams, than that which leads to the deepest recesses of her unconscious – an abyss that's right next to Shadowland.

•

In Smallwood's profile, published more than a year after Weinstein's ignominious end, Dern recounted her experiences in the shadows of Shadowland. Between the ages of twelve and sixteen, she saw and experienced firsthand 'horrifically inappropriate' behaviour on film sets. As Dern explained, 'Like, yeah, I'm doing an audition sitting on a bed with a 40-year-old filmmaker reading together a love scene, and I'm 13, but I know how to get out of this door, and I know I'm safe – but anything could have happened. What was I doing there?' That she was never assaulted she chalked up to 'mere luck'. (During an appearance on *The Ellen DeGeneres Show* that aired shortly after the Weinstein scandal broke in October 2017, however, Dern seemed to suggest that she hadn't always left these encounters unscathed.) Dern, an active member of Time's Up, a legal defence fund for victims of sexual assault and harassment founded in 2018, was working, as Smallwood notes, on changing the Screen Actors Guild audition and set rules to better protect young actors.

The Weinstein revelations have led many actresses to reassess their past. Dern has, in interviews, not only recalled the indignities she endured as a teenage performer but also reconsidered a crucial plot point in Joyce Chopra's *Smooth Talk*. The film – loosely adapted from Joyce Carol Oates's 1966 short story 'Where Are You Going, Where Have You Been?' and set in a Northern Californian suburb – features Dern in her first leading role. (The screenplay was written by Tom Cole, Chopra's husband.) She plays Connie, who spends the summer before her sophomore year in high school ogling boys at the mall with her besties ('Oh my god, it's the guys with the buns!') before advancing to make-out sessions with suitors picked up at the local hot dog stand.

Simultaneously emboldened and terrified by her own desire – 'Stop, I– I'm not used to feeling this excited,' she pleads to one stud before fleeing his car – Connie soon becomes the fixation of the much older Arnold Friend (Treat Williams), a predator who coos creepy come-ons through her screen door, ultimately enticing her to go for a ride with him. What happens between them is deliberately left open-ended. Does Arnold rape Connie? Does she have consensual sex with him? Is their encounter after she agrees to drive off with him to a secluded spot ultimately devoid of sex or sexual violence? What's not arguable is Connie's hard-won understanding of her own agency. Also indisputable is Dern's brilliance in the film: still a teenager herself at the time of *Smooth Talk*'s release and just a year away from playing the more upbeat, if more puzzling, Sandy in *Blue Velvet*, she perfectly conveys insolence, invincibility and insecurity. Writing in 1986 about the experience of seeing her story adapted, Oates was quick to praise the young actress: 'Laura Dern is so right as "my" Connie that I may come to think I modeled the fictitious girl on her, in the way that writers frequently delude themselves about notions of causality.'

Not every viewer interprets that pivotal scene the same way. Smallwood, for instance, sees less ambiguity than I do: '*Smooth Talk* strongly suggests that Dern's character is going off to be raped,' she writes. And Dern herself, almost thirty years later, seemed to have completely changed her mind about what happened in the movie. As Smallwood reports, after the film's release, Dern, in an interview, vehemently put forth her belief that Arthur and Connie simply went for a drive.

In that 1990 Q&A with Indiana, Dern told him, 'It's amazing, too, how many people said after seeing *Smooth Talk*, "Well, obviously he raped her." I think he actually did just take her for a drive.' Furthermore, Dern, at least then, five years after *Smooth Talk*'s premiere, thought of Connie as a character with some power. As she explained to Indiana,

> The line I find fascinating in *Smooth Talk* – when ... Treat says, 'Come on, you gonna come out of your daddy's house, my sweet blue-eyed girl?' – is when I reply, 'What if my eyes were brown?' ... It's like Connie's saying, 'I'm in control of this, I'm in the driver's seat.'

When Smallwood, while reporting the piece in 2018, read back Dern's initial assertion about that scene and asked her what she now thought, the actress, after a long pause, replied, 'That was my decision at the time, and I think it's because I had to be telling myself that narrative.' Might this be another way of saying, per one of Nikki's shattered selves, 'It's a story that happened yesterday. But I know it's tomorrow'? Smallwood notes that Dern's experience making

Jennifer Fox's autobiographically informed *The Tale* (2018) – in which Dern plays Fox's surrogate, a documentary filmmaker who realises that the sexual relationship she had at thirteen with her forty-year-old track coach wasn't a love affair but statutory rape – played no small part in Dern's reconsideration. (That reappraisal seems ongoing. Dern, who participated in a Zoom discussion about *Smooth Talk* held in conjunction with the movie's inclusion in the Revivals sidebar of the 2020 New York Film Festival, fulsomely praised Chopra and Oates but was quick to stress her naiveté at the time: 'I didn't know a lot of what I was enacting.')

Here I reach another semantic deadlock: how can I write about Dern enduring the sordid realities of being an actress in Hollywood without victimising her? Even trickier, how can I write about Dern revisiting, from a post-Weinstein vantage point, the films she made when she was younger without making it sound as if she is victimising *herself*? Just as crucially, how can I look slightly askance at the great, ongoing "reckoning" that has followed Weinstein's toppling, in which the more complex aspects of sexuality risk being sacrificed, without sounding as if I am in any way trying to minimise or diminish the all-too-real ubiquity of misogyny and sexual violence? Why do I flinch at the thought of Dern re-analysing the complex, ambiguous *Smooth Talk* – a film filled with uncertainties that she, eighteen when the film was released, once embraced – to fit a current orthodoxy that seems so often to insist on sexual relations, at least those between women and men, as the 'seedbed for trauma'? (Which is more traumatic: acting or heterosexuality?) Is it because I, a coeval of Dern's – we are both Gen Xers; she is eighteen months older than I am – balk at this grim, rigid view of heterosexuality, even though I have never participated in the practice?

•

'Something inside the story', *The Tale*, 'telling myself that narrative': the phrases, the title underscore the enormous power of what is told, what is passed down, whether fact or fiction. Stories are conceived as something sinister, as wound, as bad object. In his book *Victorian Hauntings*, the British literary critic and theorist Julian Wolfreys asserts that 'to tell a story is always to invoke ghosts, to open a space through which something other returns.'

Recalling the terrifying experience of his initial viewing of *Inland Empire*, alone in Lynch's private screening room in the Hollywood Hills, Lim writes in *The Man from Another Place*: 'I found eerily plausible [the film's] contention that there could be "something inside the story", as one character puts it, something malignant and possibly contagious.' Stories, narratives transmogrify into entities both pernicious and immortal. Lim continues: 'The film's queasiest special effect is in persuading the viewer that its stories – all stories – have a life of their own, that they are spaces to inhabit, forces that haunt.' To assuage Devon, increasingly skittish about continuing in the cursed *On High in Blue Tomorrows*, his unctuous agent deploys a tautology: 'Stories are stories – Hollywood's full of them.'

•

The story of Elizabeth Short – fact transmuted into sick legend and open-ended saga – haunts Hollywood, as does the story of Harvey Weinstein, an epic of debasement that looms as large as the grimmest, grimiest fairy tale. The stories told *by* the movies are sometimes as depraved as those that occur when the cameras aren't rolling. I think of the early film roles of Dern's parents. In Roger Corman's cult biker film *The Wild Angels* (1966) – during the production of which Dern was reportedly conceived – Ladd plays Gaysh, married to Loser, who is played by Bruce Dern. At Loser's funeral, Gaysh is drugged and raped by two of his Harley-riding, Nazi-worshipping confederates. In *The Rebel Rousers*, shot in January 1967, the character portrayed by a visibly pregnant Ladd is offered up by Bruce Dern's motorcycle gang leader as the spoils of victory to the winner of a drag race.

A few years earlier, in his debut credited screen performance, Bruce Dern played a character identified only as Sailor in *Marnie*. During the final act of Hitchcock's frenzied movie, as Hedren's damaged title character is recounting the traumatic incident that led to her numerous pathologies, he appears, in flashback, as one of her mother's johns, one whose sexual avidity soon turns to Marnie, then a child.

Hedren's accounts of being tormented by Hitchcock on set (and off) for both *Marnie* and *The Birds* (1963) are well known. (Also well known: the enormous influence of Hitchcock's 1958 masterwork *Vertigo*, the quintessential film about doubling, on Lynch's entire corpus.) Holding up *Marnie* like a prism, I see odd, atavistic refractions, energy waves passing through Laura Dern's film roles. In *Wild at Heart*, Sailor is also the name of Lula's lover. Tippi – the sobriquet of a real actress who endured tremendous misery inflicted by Hitchcock while playing an anguished character in *Marnie* – forms a near rhyme with Nikki, the name of a fictional actress who also suffers psychic disintegration but who is played by a performer who appears to have enjoyed a respectful, harmonious collaboration with her director. Another slant rhyme: Marnie – mad, larcenous, suicidal, single, childless mid-century woman – with Marmee, selfless, beloved, highly competent nineteenth-century matriarch.

•

Nikki begins to disintegrate when she can no longer distinguish her real self from the character she's playing; the story of Susan Blue in *On High in Blue Tomorrows* haunts her, consumes her. (Am I, indulging in all of these non sequiturs and tangents, also beginning to disintegrate?) Nikki loses the plot of her life, of the film she is making. Dern, in interviews, has tried to square an incident from her past about a fictional film she had defended – one that was largely hailed for its complexity at the time but today might be castigated, at the very least, as "problematic" – by sticking to a new script, one that increasingly disallows nuance.

Curiously, though, whenever she's been asked to reflect on the four projects she's made to date with Lynch – whose body of work, in film and television, is nearly unequalled for the squalid truths about sex and violence, especially against women, that it probes – Dern has been vague, even generous in her assessments of the more lurid aspects of his oeuvre. In an interview from 2015, two years before the Weinstein scandal, Dern said of *Blue Velvet*: 'Everyone talks about the violence and cruelty in David's films, but he's also a profound believer, and that's where the characters I've played for him have hung out; that's the part of David I have access to as an actor.' Post-Weinstein, she remains the director's champion. During an onstage discussion in December 2017, Dern called Lynch, with whom she remains close friends, 'our bravest artist working'.

Some might call that bravery brutality. One of the Nikki/Susan avatars is punched in the face twice by her husband (Peter J. Lucas), who becomes enraged when he learns that she's pregnant, for he cannot father children. (The baleful nature of her spouse, who inhabits nearly as many incarnations as Nikki does, is immediately apparent: we first see him staring down from the top of a staircase with a look of savage hate at his wife, as she and two female friends squeal with delight after Nikki finds out she got the part in *On High in Blue Tomorrows*.) Male fists also meet female faces in

Blue Velvet – 'I want you to hurt me,' Dorothy says to Jeffrey during sex – and in *Twin Peaks: The Return*. In *Wild at Heart*, Dern's Lula, who we learn was raped at thirteen by one of her father's business associates, is sexually assaulted by Bobby Peru (Willem Dafoe); turned on by the violation, she's then humiliated for her excitement.

In an email, a gay male Parisian friend asks me, 'How do you engage with Lynch gender-wise?' I write back that I am often moved by his perverse empathy, that the suffering that his abused, deranged or dead (as in the case of *Twin Peaks*' Laura Palmer) heroines endure isn't gratuitous or aestheticised. Rather, these torments reflect a simple, repugnant reality: that women are reviled. These scenes in the Lynch oeuvre are difficult to watch; sometimes I find them repellent. Yet they haunt, exposing the foul veracities of not only Hollywood but also small-town America, the world at large; each locale – any locale – perpetuates the misogyny indigenous to it. But I wonder: why has Dern distanced herself from *Smooth Talk*'s discomfiting scenes but not those in Lynch's films?

I had to be telling myself that narrative. Dern's statement rings as a corollary to a famous pronouncement of Joan Didion's: 'We tell ourselves stories in order to live.' (The line, in fact, is quoted by Dern's character in *The Tale.*) What is the story about/of Dern, about actresses, about the burdens of actresses – what they are supposed to do and say, on camera or off – in the post-Weinstein era? How much of this reckoning is itself a kind of performance? Am I failing to adequately distinguish Laura Dern the person from the spokesperson role that she has had to fulfil over the decades while promoting her films? (In that Q&A with Indiana, Dern reflected on the ways that being the daughter of Hollywood eminences helped her learn that the profession demanded much more than acting: 'I also had a good understanding about press: that it's the actor's responsibility to publicize his or her films, that the press can be fun, that it's not about hyping yourself into stardom or trying to sell yourself as a hot ticket.')

•

How many categorical errors have I committed so far? Am I conflating Dern with the parts she's played, similar to the way that Nikki collapses into Susan? Dern, as I mentioned earlier, used Catherine Deneuve's performance in *Repulsion* as a model for her own in *Inland Empire*. Deneuve, like Dern, has also been a polemical voice at home: in 1971, she added her name to the 'Manifesto of the 343 Sluts', whose signatories admitted to having an abortion, illegal in France until 1975; more infamously, in 2018 she co-sponsored a letter denouncing the country's version of #MeToo for going too far. Born twenty-four years before Dern, also to actor parents – though of the stage, not the screen – Deneuve made this blunt declaration to *Life* magazine in 1966, the year after *Repulsion*'s premiere: 'I owe my start in movies entirely to my face and body.' The statement chimes with Tomlin's 'All I have is my voice and my body... to make it believable.' But whereas Tomlin thinks of her corporeal being as one of the main tools at her disposal, to be further honed, Deneuve's assertion, made when she was only twenty-two, evinces a weary knowingness that her physicality was an asset to be exploited. Tomlin, a gay woman, thinks of herself as subject; Deneuve, a straight one, as object. Dern, in that *Times* profile at least, has portrayed herself as both.

•

What is an actress allowed to say when the cameras aren't rolling, when the words are hers and not recited from a script? In interviews, Dern has wistfully recalled the strong sorority her mother had formed with other actresses like Shelley Winters – Dern's godmother – and Jane Fonda. That distaff camaraderie was something that Dern, while growing up, had hoped to share as she became an actress with others in her profession, a female fellowship that eluded her, she has said, until only recently. Dern has summoned up this rosy tableau of Ladd's network, a kind of gathering that Dern herself has endeavoured to recreate:

> Sitting around a fireplace with a group of revolutionaries, talking about art and how the art can make a difference, how to use their voice,

> how to get in the streets, how to parent, how to single-parent and be an actress, how to navigate relationships and intimacy through all of it.

I am brought up short by 'a group of revolutionaries'. The term would certainly be applicable to Fonda, especially in the seventies, the decade of Dern's childhood, when she may have seen Fonda sitting around a fireplace and when Dern made her first onscreen appearances. The seventies were also the years when Fonda – daughter of one of golden-era Hollywood's most revered actors, and sister of one the foundational figures of New American Cinema (Peter Fonda, in fact, starred with Ladd and Bruce Dern in *The Wild Angels*) – became the movie industry's most politically outspoken, if not committed, star, owing mainly to her steadfast opposition to the Vietnam War. (In Hal Ashby's *Coming Home*, a 1978 movie set during that war but debuting three years after its end, Fonda plays the dutiful spouse of Bruce Dern's tyrannical marine corps captain, who oversees carnage in Southeast Asia.)

Fonda remains the paradigm of how – if it's even possible – to reconcile the committed civilian with the celebrity. Of her many attackers during this era, perhaps none were as insidious as Jean-Luc Godard and Jean-Pierre Gorin; near the end of their acidic 1972 essay film *Letter to Jane*, a semiotic scrutiny of a photo of a stern-faced Fonda meeting with North Vietnamese citizens in Hanoi, Gorin delivers this icy indictment: 'One must realise that stars aren't allowed to think.'

I am not certain whom Dern would consider a group of revolutionaries among her peers – the cast of *Big Little Lies*? I don't wish to disparage Dern for her earnestness or to subject her to a Godard/Gorin level of condescension. But when she mentions 'talking about art and how the art can make a difference' as one of the goals of her engagé actress community, I wonder which of her films and TV shows she would place in that exalted category. Does 'art' include *The Tale*, a blunt work of psychotherapeutic ejecta that demands Dern be strident and outraged in every scene? Does it exclude *Smooth Talk*, a project that more intelligently and sensitively addresses female sexuality and desire and one that, to my mind, refuses to see its protagonist as a victim?

Does it include *Enlightened*, the short-lived HBO show she co-created with Mike White, in which she stars as a woman who, zealous in her efforts to be an 'agent of change', alienates and jeopardises those she wishes to help?

Does 'art' include or exclude the projects she's done with Lynch, works that promulgate no political stance, that can never easily be reconciled with the mandates of #MeToo, that honour only the extreme reaches of their maker's unconscious? Works like *Twin Peaks: The Return*, which gave Dern a multifaceted role but also occasioned a host of predictably scolding reviews, such as the one that sniffed in its syntactically disastrous lede, 'There's a moment in the new season of *Twin Peaks* where it becomes clear that after more than three decades making movies and TV, David Lynch still has a prominent male gaze'? Works especially like *Inland Empire*, which abounds with scenes of female abjection – episodes, full of twisted compassion, that perversely yet powerfully highlight the immiserations attendant to being an actress, to being a woman – and which stands as a project that is as much a creation of the woman in front of the camera as of the man behind it?

'I gouged a man's eye out when I was fifteen once; he was tryin' to rape me,' the Avenging Angel says in her monologue. Connie, in *Smooth Talk*, is also fifteen. Connie may also have fended off a rapist. At the end of Chopra's movie, when Connie tells her older sister about the incident with Arnold Friend – which occurred while Connie, having refused to join her family on a picnic, was alone – she equivocates, assures, dissembles: 'This man, he came and asked me for a ride. And I went. ... Maybe I didn't go. Maybe I'm going out of my mind. I... Listen, I didn't go. Don't worry. It didn't even happen.' Connie's words are addled. She loses the plot. Connie's words to her sibling prefigure those of the Avenging Angel to the ineffectual man with smeary glasses: 'The thing is, I don't know what was before or after.'

•

Like the Avenging Angel, I often don't know what was before or after in *Inland Empire* no matter how many times I've watched it. Recursive episodes proliferate in the film. At least three times Nikki/Susan dissociates, looking at another version of herself from another vantage point. The Avenging Angel enters an empty movie palace, here a de facto hall of mirrors: she sees herself onscreen saying, 'Watchin' it, like in a dark theatre.'

That nearly vacant cinema instantly recalls *Mulholland Drive*'s Club Silencio, the mystical cabaret that Betty and Rita, desire-drunk after having sex, cab to in the middle of the night – and where their love story, if not their very identities, begins to unravel. But while revisiting *Inland Empire*, I begin to see repetition, connections across not only Lynch's but Dern's filmography – and to the gruesome history of Shadowland. 'Where did you go? Where have you been?' the Greek chorus asks Nikki/Susan after she appears on Hollywood Boulevard, or, more accurately, after she's back, following a time/space detour, on that street *again*, where she will die, soaked in her own blood. Their query closely matches 'Where Are You Going, Where Have You Been?', the title of the Oates short story – inspired by the real-life Pied Piper of Tucson, a serial seducer and murderer of young women in the mid-sixties – on which *Smooth Talk* is based.

Interiors are also echoed, refracted. Dorothy's residence in the Deep River Apartments complex in *Blue Velvet* is designed to destabilise; her one-bedroom flat 'appears to have been furnished, not to mention lit and photographed, to fulfill the surrealist ambition of making everyday objects strange,' as Lim writes. Living spaces also estrange, derange in *Inland Empire*. Often shot in distorting wide angles, the enormous rooms of Nikki's Hollywood mansion – replete with marble columns, Persian rugs the size of football fields, and ornate Louis XV-style furniture – seem suffused with dread. Their cavernousness reminds me of one of the more infamous two-page photo spreads in *Hollywood Babylon*: the trashed suite of San Francisco's luxury St. Francis Hotel where silent film star Roscoe 'Fatty' Arbuckle held, in 1921, a bacchanal to celebrate a new, lucrative contract with Paramount. The revelry led to a seismic scandal in the movie industry. One of the guests, an aspiring actress named Virginia Rappe, died a few days after the party. (Her ghastly demise would seem to anticipate Elizabeth Short's twenty-six years later.) Arbuckle was arraigned on charges of manslaughter, and rumours spread of his using champagne bottles (and other objects) to rape Rappe. Unlike another hulking man, Harvey Weinstein, Arbuckle was eventually acquitted, after three trials. But despite being legally cleared of wrongdoing, Fatty, like Harvey, was shunned and unemployable, a pariah.

Diabolical décor also dominates the shabby house where one of the Nikki/Susan avatars lives. Its shag carpet is a vomitous green; lamps, emitting a sickly incarnadine glow, especially seem gravid with sinister powers, much as they are in *Mulholland Drive*. This tumbledown one-storey home somewhere in Southern California, its exterior sooty and stained, recalls, in turn, the modest dwelling of Connie and her family – which has been in a state of disarray for several years, as various renovation projects remain unfinished – in the northern part of the state in *Smooth Talk*.

Connie's bedroom, like that of teenagers everywhere, is a makeshift shrine. Her fetish objects are eclectic. Her panda bear figurines slightly outnumber her multiple posters of James Dean, a brooding heartthrob (one whom Arnold Friend tries to emulate) and a famous disciple of the Actors Studio, just like Montgomery Clift, whose damaged visage – stitched and reassembled after a car crash in 1956 that nearly killed him – assumes pride of place in Sandy's bedroom in *Blue Velvet*. Clift's terror-stricken mug tells a story, presaging the look of unremitting horror and dread that creeps across Nikki/Susan's face as it pushes up against the camera. That face – Dern's rubberised, weaponised face – articulates the story of *Inland Empire* most succinctly and cohesively.

•

Characters are nested within and 'leak out of' Nikki. Similarly, stories are nested within *Inland Empire*. In addition to *On High in Blue Tomorrows*, there is the austere sitcom "starring" the rabbit-human crossbreeds played by Watts, Harring and Coffey that takes place on a set that suggests *Father Knows Best* by way of Fassbinder. Running throughout *Inland Empire* are references to Axxon N., identified by a tinny off-screen voice at the very beginning of the movie as 'the longest-running radio play in history.' 'Axxon N.' appears, graffiti-like, on walls, in alleyways. Nikki/Susan spots the bizarre proper noun on a decaying metal door, underscored with an arrow pointing to an entryway; she follows the sign and finds herself in a wormhole, transported back in time to an early rehearsal of *On High in Blue Tomorrows*, a run-through taking place on a Paramount soundstage. Later, the Avenging Angel catches a glance of this cryptic term on Hollywood Boulevard.

Could Axxon N. be the actual story, the sprawling narrative of the three-hour *Inland Empire*? Does Axxon derive from 'axon', defined by Merriam-Webster as 'a usually long and single nerve-cell process that usually conducts impulses away from the cell body'? Thinking of that extra 'x' in Axxon, I remember that the letter, in algebra, means a value that is not yet known, a variable – a quantity that changes, just like Nikki.

•

But I'm losing the plot again. Free-associating like this is my desperate way of trying to make sense of a film that continuously defies it, that is itself a product of free association. I go back to what Dern told me over the phone fifteen years ago: 'There was clearly a mystery, as there always is – there's a mystery to solve as the actor in the story.' Dern, as Sandy in *Blue Velvet*, helps solve a mystery; she dances, in a wood-panelled suburban rec room, with Jeffrey to Julee Cruise's 'Mysteries of Love'. To watch Dern's sleuthing, her guesswork 'as the actor in the story' in *Inland Empire* is to gain traction in a project designed to elude our grasp. 'Motion pictures are for people who like to watch women,' McDonald wrote, his words providing a spot-on credo for this dyke cinephile. McDonald composed several impassioned paeans to actresses but, unlike me, he did not desire women; a caveat to his aesthetic principle about cinema spectatorship is this more personal avowal: 'May I say that I like women better than men, but not for cock.'

A few years ago, in response to my ardour for *Mulholland Drive*, which I have always praised as a great lesbian love story, a sapphic friend of otherwise excellent taste and judgment dismissed the film as too 'male gaze-y', making a cumbersome term all the more cudgel-like by turning it into an adjective. I recall something that Patricia White wrote in 1999: 'Feminist film theory has been unable to envision women who looked at women with desire,' an assessment that still largely remains true more than twenty years later – not just in film theory but in popular culture, where the equally reductive term 'the female gaze' has taken hold.

Liking to watch women does not always mean desiring them, even if a spectator desires women in general. But at the very least, to like to watch women onscreen means to be deeply interested, invested in what they do. It means, regardless of your gender or sexuality, to be a voyeur, a term that I do not use damningly and that need not be incompatible with a spectator's identification as a feminist. As the film scholar and critic Erika Balsom so astutely pointed out – vis-à-vis a discussion of Bette Gordon's *Variety* (1983) in a 2020 article about the limitations of the use of 'the female gaze' as a rubric – voyeurism

> is an integral part of psychic life, a terrain of struggle far too important for feminism to vacate. ... [*Variety*] recognizes that there can be power and pleasure in being an object, that the field of the gaze will always be marked by dynamic asymmetries, and that women are scopophiles, too.

Illustrating Balsom's piercing observation, two characters in *Inland Empire* stand out as spell-bound female spectators: the weeping Lost Girl, who cannot tear herself away from the images on her hotel TV, and the Avenging Angel, who stands transfixed, if puzzled, by her own depiction on an enormous movie screen. (At one point, the former implores, 'Cast out this wicked dream that has seized my heart,' an oblique homage to Billy Wilder's *Sunset Boulevard*, a frequent Lynch touchstone. The 1950 meta-film features

Gloria Swanson as an ageing, imperious actress named Norma Desmond, among cinema's most entranced female viewers. Norma is besotted with revisiting her earlier movies – in this instance 1932's *Queen Kelly*, which starred Swanson, and a line from which the Lost Girl's prayer replicates.) Maybe McDonald's maxim could be amended to *motion pictures are for people who like to watch women watching.*

To continue Balsom's assertion about the 'power and pleasure in being an object', I'd add that, in the case of Dern, there is power and pleasure in performing instability, disintegration, abjection – and power and pleasure in *witnessing* how she paradoxically exerts such control while falling apart. As a kind of reward, perhaps, for Dern's fortitude (not to mention that of the audience), *Inland Empire* surprisingly ends ecstatically; as Lim points out, the film 'is almost all nightmare, and yet, through considerable exertions, it blinks itself awake, and into a state of grace.' The penultimate sequence finds the Avenging Angel and the Lost Girl in a tender embrace. Each is then restored to some version of happiness, or, at the very least, equilibrium, their actions accompanied by the ethereal 'Polish Poem', a track sung by Chrysta Bell, which she wrote with Lynch.

In the concluding scene, in a boutique hotel lobby, we see a beaming Nikki – though I am tempted to write 'Dern', for the woman who sits before us in this segment exhibits none of the postures or mannerisms of Nikki or any of her personae. The look on her face recalls Sandy's wide-eyed wonder as she discusses the 'blinding light of love' in *Blue Velvet*. Throughout the closing credits sequence, Dern, after that flirty exchange with Harring described earlier, looks skyward. She never even turns to her seatmate, just a foot or two away on a sofa: Nastassja Kinski.

While her fleeting presence is yet another of *Inland Empire*'s mysteries, we might think of Kinski as a European analogue of Dern. Though six years older than the American actress, she was also born to actors – her father, Klaus Kinski, being far more notorious than her mother, Ruth Brigitte Tocki. Nastassja made her screen debut in 1975, as the mute, sexually precocious

Mignon in Wim Wenders's *Wrong Move*, a film that premiered when she was fourteen – just a year older than Dern was when *Foxes* was released. (As the title heroine of 1979's *Tess*, Nastassja also has a connection to another of Shadowland's personages: Polanski, whose indirect tie to *Inland Empire* I noted earlier.)

•

During the long instrumental build-up to Nina Simone's galvanic 1965 cover of the traditional spiritual 'Sinnerman' – six scorching minutes of which score *Inland Empire*'s final credits – the Greek chorus enters the lobby and performs a tentative line dance. (Earlier in the film they had gyrated with more enthusiasm to Little Eva's 'The Loco-Motion' and Etta James's 'At Last'.) But soon they, and nearly everyone else in the hotel lobby, Dern included, are eclipsed by a septet of Black women dancers, led by Monique Cash, who alone lip-synchs Simone's vocals. Although their faces are sometimes obscured by scrolling text, their movements are exultant, propulsive, embodying the word that Simone sings repeatedly near the end of the song: *power*.

Their jubilant appearance in this benighted epic somehow isn't incongruous. What their presence underscores, though, is absence – that is, how few Black performers can be found in Lynch's oeuvre. When they do appear, they are frequently relegated to brief, often abased roles, such as the unnamed homeless woman (portrayed by the non-professional performer Helena Chase) who offers cold comfort to Nikki/Susan as she vomits blood near Hollywood and Vine: 'It's okay. You dyin', is all.' (She is one of two anonymous Black people living on the street in *Inland Empire*. The other is played by Terry Crews, then best known for his role as the salt-of-the-earth dad on the sitcom *Everybody Hates Chris*. In October 2017, he would become one of the first men in Hollywood to detail his sexual assault, in this instance by a male talent agency executive.)

When I first saw *Inland Empire*, at a New York Film Festival press screening in late September 2006 – before Lynch had avowed that this would be his last movie – the final sequence with the dancers struck me as an act of atonement, a compensatory (but, to be clear, not token) acknowledgment of the paucity of Black performers in his corpus. I wondered whether the film would mark a year zero, signalling a new direction in Lynch's forthcoming work. As Jacques Rivette said of his gargantuan *Out 1: Noli me tangere* (1971), which, like *Inland Empire*, is also about the bewilderments of performing and the ever-unstable boundary between fantasy and reality, 'the fiction ... gobbles everything up, and finally it self-destructs.' (The French director's comment recalls the metaphoric maw summoned by Toles: 'A moving-picture image somehow acquires enough living dimension to swallow the credulous viewer whole.') I imagine Dern's pliant mouth devouring *Inland Empire*, if not all of Lynch's work to date. His output consumed, the writer-director could begin de novo.

Yet when Lynch's next major undertaking, *Twin Peaks: The Return*, premiered nearly eleven years later, the rousing finale of *Inland Empire* proved more anomalous than auguring. In the series' eighteen episodes, I can recall only one named Black character: Jade (Nafessa Williams), a sex worker in Las Vegas who services MacLachlan's Dougie Jones. The role is dispiritingly narrow, its flimsiness all the more disappointing considering the scores of densely detailed characters, major and minor, that populate the series.

But speaking of flimsy: I don't want this criticism of Lynch to sound simplified or reproving, nor do I want to subject *Inland Empire* or any of his projects to blunt sociological data points, tallying up a balance sheet and finding his oeuvre in arrears. Lynch – like any other artist – cannot, and should not be expected to, redress social ills. The discussion of race in his films has been ongoing since at least 1997, the year David Foster Wallace asked 'why are Lynch's movies all so *white*?' (The limits of Wallace's answer – that Lynch's world view is inherently 'apolitical' – were highlighted in 2018 when the director stated that Trump 'could go down as one of the greatest presidents in history because he has disrupted the thing so much.' In response to Lynch's comments, Lim wrote, 'They are irksome not because they endorse Trump – as numerous headlines falsely declared – but because they represent the privileged position of distance. Lynch, needless to say, is insulated from, and perhaps oblivious to, the most cruel and backward of Trump's policies.')

If Black people remain largely absent from Lynch's filmography, perhaps that's because the dominant and abiding theme in his work is the pathologies of whiteness. As the critic Sarah Nicole Prickett, writing about *Twin Peaks: The Return* for *Artforum* online, noted, 'Lynch specializes in a whiteness that slips from the norm, from seats of power, from centers that are traditionally but never essentially, exclusively white, to become whiteness per se.' Nikki and her many splintered selves, plummeting deeper into degradation, exemplify this motif.

•

Most of the first draft of this monograph was written between March and August 2020, when reality seemed as fractured and terrifying as the way that Nikki/Susan experiences it. Before lockdown, I knew that the Inland Empire was an actual place but most strongly associated those two words with the title of Lynch's final movie. But while I was working on this small book, the Southern California region would come to represent another kind of nightmare. On July 9, 2020 – around the time when Covid-19 cases began surging in the South and West of the US, which would see almost two million new infections that month alone – the *New York Times* published a piece on rising coronavirus cases in the Inland Empire. That increase was attributed to spread among low-wage warehouse employees for behemoths like Amazon and Walmart – a labour force in which Latinx and Black workers are over-represented. 'The spike comes as Americans continue to rely on e-commerce giants to deliver their necessities as the pandemic drags on,' the article notes. 'That means the need for people to sort, package, ship and deliver goods has grown, along with demand for the warehouses and fulfillment centers where that work can be done.'

Once known as an area 'where many lower income, immigrant parents could afford to buy houses with yards after living in cramped Los Angeles apartments,' the region is now glutted with fifty-two million square metres of industrial space. I wonder whether the house where Nikki/Susan resides, in a section of what I envision to be the Inland Empire, still stands – the site of a backyard cookout that quickly turns morbid when her husband's white T-shirt becomes covered with ketchup, a smear of red that evokes all the blood that will be shed in the movie. *Inland Empire*, a film from 2006, tracks an actress having a psychotic break. In 2020, the real Inland Empire proved to be illustrative of the multiple psychoses afflicting the United States: a rampaging virus, festering racism, a brutal economic system, a rapacious logistics industry, environmental desecration.

•

Paradoxically, the man whose films have instilled so much dread and unease has recently devoted himself to producing microdoses of balm. Starting May 11, 2020, Lynch began posting to YouTube daily weather reports for the Los Angeles area, each lasting about forty-five to ninety seconds. Their very ordinariness makes them oddly pacifying; they are not unlike the Conceptual artist On Kawara's 'Today' series (1966–2013), paintings that consist solely of the date on which they were created. In each video, Lynch, who appears to be broadcasting from a basement room or bunker, wears the same black dress shirt, buttoned to the top; his outfit is as unvarying as Southern California weather. (As of early 2021, though, his luxuriant snowy mane and facial hair have waxed and waned, and he's been accessorising with sunglasses.) After announcing the day and date for each dispatch, he notes the morning's current temperature and the likely high, figures presented in both Fahrenheit and Celsius. Often he predicts 'beautiful blue skies and golden sunshine'. Each post ends with Lynch giving a small salute and wishing viewers to 'have a great day'. His low-key jovial demeanour in these quotidian updates has provided a smidge of comfort amid so much death, illness and anxiety. They remind us of the astonishing fact that the sun has risen, at least once more.

This is not the first time Lynch has offered weather bulletins. He inaugurated these daily dispatches in the mid-2000s, posting them to davidlynch.com, a site no longer extant. Almost always the lone person in front of the camera, Lynch, for the February 1, 2005 report – a date during which *Inland Empire* would have been in some stage of production – had a guest: Dern, who sat to the director's right. Black sunglasses pushed up on her head, the actress, wordless, held a piece of paper with 'FEB. 1' written on it, though the inverse of the abbreviated date is what we see. At the very end of this 36-second clip, she smiles slightly.

Lynch may be the only one talking in that meteorology memo, but it is Dern who commands our attention; the rise and fall of her chest as she breathes gives the clip its rhythm and shape. In this prosaic notice of less than a minute, she reveals the qualities that have made her indispensable to his oeuvre, not least *Inland Empire*, a phantasmagoric epic that she anchors with definition, exactitude. ‘Here in Los Angeles, it’s a beautiful sunny day, not a cloud in the sky,’ he blares. His silent partner is on high in blue tomorrows – not cursed but sublime.

10 *evil twin* – Manohla Dargis, 'The Trippy Dream Factory of David Lynch', *New York Times* (online) (6 December 2006)

12 *describe* – Chris Rodley, *Lynch on Lynch: Revised Edition*, ed. Chris Rodley (New York: Farrar, Straus and Giroux, 2005), 266

13 *words are the movie's enemy* – Rodley, 266

13 *put things in words* – David Lynch, quoted in Dennis Lim, 'David Lynch Returns: Expect Moody Conditions, With Surreal Gusts', *New York Times* (online) (1 October 2006)

15 *it was Dern who supplied the film with its title* – David Lynch, *Catching the Big Fish: Meditation, Consciousness, and Creativity* (New York: Jeremy P. Tarcher, 2006), 143

16 *acteurism* – Dave Kehr, programme notes for 'Acteurism: The Emergence of Ann Sheridan, 1937–1943', Museum of Modern Art (online) (October 2014)

16 *devoted to actors* – Kehr

17 *importance of the movie star* – Boyd McDonald, *Cruising the Movies: A Sexual Guide to Oldies on TV* (South Pasadena: Semiotext(e), 2015), 142

18 *films depend on a form of communication* – James Naremore, *Acting in the Cinema* (Berkeley: University of California Press, 1988), 2

18 *a series of expressive techniques* – Naremore, 4

20 *motion pictures* – Boyd McDonald, quoted in William E. Jones, 'Introduction', McDonald, *Cruising the Movies*, 20

20 *the actor's life* – David Lynch, quoted in Dennis Lim, 'Gone Fishin'', *The Village Voice* (online) (9 October 2001)

24 *he was looking for someone* – Laura Dern, quoted in Hannah Lack, 'Laura Dern Is an Actor at the Height of Her Power', *AnOther Magazine* (online) (2 February 2020)

33 *the only earthly identity* – George Toles, 'Auditioning Betty in *Mulholland Drive*', *Film Quarterly* 58, no. 1 (Fall 2004), 13n1

37 *rife with contradictions* – Toles, 11

37 *full throttle romantic acting* – Toles, 11–12

39 *trancelike* – Laura Dern, quoted in Kristine McKenna, 'The Happiest of Happy Endings', Lynch and McKenna, *Room to Dream*, 416

41 *never saw any whole, W-H-O-L-E* – Lynch, quoted in Lim, 'David Lynch Returns'

43 *unbelievably freeing* – Laura Dern, quoted in Lim

43 *playing a broken or dismantled person* – Dern, quoted in Lim

44 *pattern of role confusion* – Toles, 'Auditioning Betty in *Mulholland Drive*', 10

45 *realist acting* – Naremore, *Acting in the Cinema*, 72

46 *clearly a mystery* – Laura Dern, conversation with the author (November 2006)

47 *some actresses are stymied* – Christine Smallwood, 'Laura Dern Embraces the Messiness of Human Life', *The New York Times Magazine* (online) (7 May 2019)

48 *unbearably vulnerable* – Smallwood

48 *messy* – Smallwood

48 *deeply flawed* – Sloane Crosley, 'Laura Dern's Moment', *Vanity Fair* 702 (February 2019), 43

49 *dear Inner Self* – Sandra Seacat, quoted in Smallwood, 'Laura Dern Embraces the Messiness of Human Life'

49 *perform rituals* – Smallwood, 'Laura Dern Embraces the Messiness of Human Life'

49 *a shaman* – Sandra Seacat, quoted in 'Laura Dern and Sandra Seacat: Hollywood Mentors' [video], *The Hollywood Reporter* (online) (18 February 2015)

49 *just so beautiful* – Laura Dern, quoted in Scott Feinberg, 'Oscars: Rediscovering Laura Dern, the Actors' Actor (Q&A)', *The Hollywood Reporter* (online) (29 December 2014)

50 *Garbo offered to one's gaze*– Roland Barthes, *Mythologies*, trans. Annette Lavers (New York: The Noonday Press – Farrar, Straus & Giroux, 1972), 56

51 *to watch her* – Kenneth Tynan, 'Garbo', *Sight & Sound* 23, no. 4 (April–June 1954), 189

51 *high school boy's dream* – McDonald, *Cruising the Movies*, 92

51 *charted the territory* – Gary Indiana, 'Laura Dern', *Interview* (September 1990); republished as 'Laura Dern: New Again', *Interview* (online) (10 May 2016)

52 *still inexplicable primitive rite* – Toles, 'Auditioning Betty in *Mulholland Drive*', 12

52 *acquires enough living dimension* – Toles, 12

53 *cinema is public fantasy* – Patricia White, *Uninvited: Classical Hollywood Cinema and Lesbian Representability* (Bloomington: Indiana University Press, 1999), xv

53 *tribute* – E. Alex Jung, 'Laura Dern Doesn't Need Our Approval: But we gave her an honorary degree anyway', *Vulture* (online) (2 December 2019)

56 *Babylon-ian aspects* – Nick Pinkerton, 'Switchback: On David Lynch's 1997 Lost Highway', *Employee Picks* (blog) (25 June 2020)

57 *the Dahlia's connection with the movie industry* – Kenneth Anger, *Hollywood Babylon II* (New York and Scarborough: Plume, New American Library, 1984), 132

59 *man-crazy adventuress* – 'Police Seeking Former Marine in L.A. Slaying', *The Hanford Sentinel* (18 January 1947), 1

59 *loved to prowl* – Linda Rohr, quoted in 'Black Dahlia's Love Life Traced in Search for Her Fiendish Murderer', *The Los Angeles Times* (18 January 1947), 3

62 *the inescapable belief* – David Blum, 'The Conception, Production and Distribution of Julia Ormond', *The New York Times Magazine* (online) (9 April 1995)

62 *the next Audrey Hepburn* – John Heilpern, 'Empire of the Stage', *Vanity Fair* 423 (November 1995), 219

64 *it's hard to say exactly* – David Lynch, 'Wrapped in Plastic', in David Lynch and Kristine McKenna, *Room to Dream* (Melbourne: Text Publishing, 2018), 272

65 *judged by how we treat our fellow man* – David Lynch, quoted in Zack Sharf, 'David Lynch Reacts to Hollywood Sexual Harassment By Evoking the Golden Rule', *Indiewire* (online) (17 December 2017)

67 *a character's conspicuous fabrication* – Toles, 'Auditioning Betty in *Mulholland Drive*', 4

68 *horrifically inappropriate* – Laura Dern, quoted in Smallwood, 'Laura Dern Embraces the Messiness of Human Life'

68 *I'm doing an audition* – Dern, quoted in Smallwood

68 *mere luck* – Dern, quoted in Smallwood

68 *appearance on The Ellen DeGeneres Show* – Alyssa Bailey, 'Laura Dern Reveals She Has Been Sexually Harassed and Assaulted', *Elle* (online) (18 October 2017)

70 *so right as 'my' Connie* – Joyce Carol Oates, 'When Characters From The Page Are Made Flesh On Screen', *New York Times* (online) (23 March 1986)

70 *Smooth Talk strongly suggests* – Smallwood, 'Laura Dern Embraces the Messiness of Human Life'

71 *it's amazing* – Laura Dern, quoted in Indiana, 'Laura Dern'

71 *my decision at the time* – Dern, quoted in Smallwood, 'Laura Dern Embraces the Messiness of Human Life'

72 *I didn't know* – Laura Dern, quoted in 'NYFF58 Talk: Smooth Talk with Laura Dern, Joyce Chopra, and Joyce Carol Oates' [video], Film at Lincoln Center (online) (24 September 2020)

74 *to invoke ghosts* – Julian Wolfreys, *Victorian Hauntings: Spectrality, Gothic, the Uncanny and Literature* (Hampshire and New York: Palgrave, 2002), 3

74 *eerily plausible* – Dennis Lim, *David Lynch: The Man from Another Place* (New York: Amazon Publishing, 2015), 175–176

78 *everyone talks about* – Laura Dern, quoted in Kristine McKenna, 'A Suburban Romance, Only Different', Lynch and McKenna, *Room to Dream*, 208

78 *our bravest artist working* – Laura Dern, quoted in 'An Evening With Laura Dern' [video], Film at Lincoln Center (online) (28 December 2017)

80 *we tell ourselves stories* – Joan Didion, 'The White Album', *The White Album* (New York: Simon and Schuster, 1979), 11

80 *good understanding about press* – Dern, quoted in Indiana, 'Laura Dern'

81 *Manifesto of the 343* – 'Le Manifeste des 343. Avortement. Notre ventre nous appartient', *Le nouvel observateur* 334, no. 5 (April 1971), 5–6

81 *a letter denouncing* – 'Nous défendons une liberté d'importuner, indispensable à la liberté sexuelle', *Le Monde* (online) (9 January 2018)

81 *I owe my start* – Catherine Deneuve, quoted in 'Common Market's Glamor Stock', *Life* 60, no. 4 (28 January 1966), 47

82 *sitting around a fireplace* – Dern, quoted in Smallwood, 'Laura Dern Embraces the Messiness of Human Life'

85 *prominent male gaze* – Carli Velocci, 'Twin Peaks: The Return Proves David Lynch Still Has a Woman Problem (Commentary)', *The Wrap* (online) (31 May 2017)

88 *appears to have been furnished* – Lim, *The Man from Another Place*, 70

88 *the trashed suite* – Kenneth Anger, *Hollywood Babylon* (London: Arrow Books, 1975), 26–27

93 *I like women better* – McDonald, *Cruising the Movies*, 202

93 *feminist film theory has been unable* – White, *Uninvited*, 72

94 *voyeurism is an integral part of psychic life* – Erika Balsom, 'In Search of the Female Gaze', *Cinema Scope* 83 (Summer 2020), 40

95 *almost all nightmare* – Lim, *The Man from Another Place*, 176

99 *the fiction gobbles everything up* – Jacques Rivette, quoted in Bernard Eisenschitz, Jean-André Fieschi and Eduardo de Gregorio, 'Entretien avec Jacques Rivette', *La Nouvelle Critique* 63, no. 244 (April 1973), 68–69; translated by Giovanni Marchini Camia

100 *why are Lynch's movies all so white* – David Foster Wallace, 'David Lynch keeps his head', *A Supposedly Fun Thing I'll Never Do Again* (Boston: Little, Brown, 1997), 189

100 *Trump could go down* – David Lynch, quoted in Rory Carroll, 'David Lynch: "You gotta be selfish. It's a terrible thing"', *The Guardian* (online) (23 June 2018)

100 *irksome* – Dennis Lim, 'Donald Trump's America and the Visions of David Lynch', *The New Yorker* (online) (29 June 2018)

101 *Lynch specializes in a whiteness* – Sarah Nicole Prickett, 'Eternal Return', *Artforum* (online) (23 May 2017)

102 *the spike comes* – Jill Cowan, 'Warehouse Workers in a Bind as Virus Spikes in Southern California', *New York Times* (online) (9 July 2020)

Thank you,
Annabel Brady-Brown, Leah Gilliam, Dennis Lim, Jean Ma, Giovanni Marchini Camia, Nick Pinkerton, Vincent Sallé, Ariel Schrag, Christine Smallwood

Other titles in the Decadent Editions:

2003

Goodbye, Dragon Inn

Nick Pinkerton

2004

TEN SKIES

Erika Balsom

Forthcoming:

2005

Tale of Cinema

Dennis Lim

2008

The Headless Woman

Rebecca Harkins-Cross

Also from Fireflies Press:

Memoria

Apichatpong Weerasethakul

A chronicle of the genesis and creation of *Memoria*, the new film by Apichatpong Weerasethakul.

Printed in a beautiful art book edition, collected materials from the film's writing, pre-production and shoot offer an extraordinary immersion into the creative processes and work methods of one of contemporary cinema's true visionaries.

About the author:
Melissa Anderson is the film editor of *4Columns*. From 2015 to 2017, she was the senior film critic for the *Village Voice*. She is a frequent contributor to *Artforum* and *Bookforum*.